DRAG QUEEN DETECTIVE: SIDE SLEUTHS

CORY AND JENSEN

SHANE K MORTON

Copyright © 2022 by Shane K Morton

All Rights Reserved.

No part of this book may be reproduced in any form or by any electronic or mechanical means, including information storage and retrieval systems, without written permission from the author, except for the brief quotations in a book review.

Names, **characters**, businesses, places, events, and incidents are either the products of the author's imagination or used in a **fictitious** manner. Any resemblance to actual persons, living or dead, or actual events is purely coincidental.

Cover art © 2021 by Winterheart Design, winterheart.com

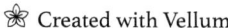 Created with Vellum

1

"That ride was wild!" Jensen was way too excited about a helicopter ride that almost killed us. He had talked the pilot into taking us through the mountain range instead of over the lake. Our host, Blake, had promised me a quick and smooth trip over the large lake, but Jensen had somehow turned this into an episode of a Bear Grylls' survival show. I had no idea that coming to Point Pleasant would be this terrifying. I wanted to scream out the score to Chicago to drown out my impeding sense of doom as we brushed through the mountainous valleys.

I'd slap the pilot, but he was apparently the only way to get home.

I was just glad Victor hadn't come with us. He hated helicopters with a passion. Of course, Jensen would have never dared to suggest a trip through the mountains if our bosses and best friends, Victor and Harper, had been here. I'd have to have a very firm discussion with him once we got to Blake's cabin. His sense of adventure was very different than mine. I preferred a sale at Macy's to crashing into a mountain peak.

"Wasn't it wild, honey?" His handsome face turned to me, and I slowly unclasped every muscle in my body. I felt safer now that we were landing on the helicopter pad in the middle of town.

"Wild?" I turned to him and tried to keep some kind of gay composure. "Wild is a night of debauchery on a stripper pole where you throw dollar bills at me. Wild is being handcuffed to the bed while you tickle me with a feather, and I can't catch my breath. This was Aargh!" I lost my composure. It really shouldn't come as a surprise to anyone who actually knew me.

I heard the pilot chuckle. Maybe I *should* slap him.

"Cory, baby... You like roller coasters." He looked so dumbfounded that I didn't know whether to kiss him or take off my engagement ring and throw it at his face. Of course, I would never do that.

"That is not the same thing." I gasped.

"Did we just have our first fight?" He reached over and took my face in his palm. I couldn't help myself – I leaned into his hand. His touch was my everything – and when he looked at me with those amazing brown eyes of his, I melted. He made me feel so loved and secure that I had to remind myself that we almost died in a fiery blaze on the side of the mountain just a few minutes ago.

"I'll let you know when we're fighting. That was foreplay." I snapped but couldn't stop myself from grinning as I suppressed the chuckle that threatened to escape. "Have we fucking landed yet? Jesus! How long does it take?"

"I'll make sure the trip back is as boring as I can make it. Promise." The pilot yelled as the helicopter touched down with a jarring yet semi-comfortable landing.

"You better," I replied, as snarky as I could. I admit it

wasn't one of my best comebacks. I was still trying to slow down the thundering of my heart.

Jensen unbuckled his safety belt and started to reach over for mine. I slapped his hand gently and reached down to undo my own. He stuck out his bottom lip and waited, a sly smile slowly spreading upon his overly handsome face. I fumbled with the latch and sighed, removing my hands from the metal buckle and allowing Jensen to reach over once again and swiftly pop me free from the restraint.

"You push down and pull, baby." His chuckle made my toes curl. Everything about Tom Jensen made me giddy with feels. He had a power over me, and I relished losing myself under that power daily. He was perfect, and he was mine. Sometimes, I pinched myself to make sure this wasn't just a fantasy I had concocted because of too much vodka and a marathon rewatch of The Golden Girls. If it was – I had never woken up.

"Thank you for gaysplaining it to me." I stuck out my tongue, and his hand lingered on my thigh.

"You shouldn't tease a man who's crazy for you. I might have to ask the pilot to take us back up again." The smirk was too much.

"Get me off this fucking helicopter, now." I reached down and took his hand in mine. He grabbed the large duffel bag that we were sharing. If I had been left to my own devices, I would have packed much differently. One never knows what they might need on a trip, and I liked to come prepared. But Tom talked me into packing lightly since we were only going to be here a few days. It must be love.

"Blake said it would be warm, and he was right." Jensen slid onto the ground and held up his muscular arms to me. I placed my hands on his shoulders as he gently helped me down from the deafening helicopter. "See you later. Thanks for the ride."

The pilot waved, and we walked down the sidewalk and towards the street. The helicopter noisily lifted back into the air and headed towards the lake that surrounded one side of the town. It made my hair a crow's nest. Perhaps I would slap the pilot when I saw him again.

Point Pleasant was way too cute!

I had noticed how adorable the town was in between squinting and praying that we wouldn't crash when we came in for our landing. Now, with my feet on firm ground, I glanced around the quaint mountain village and sighed happily. This place looked like it had been ripped out of a Hallmark movie. The buildings had a charm that only came from being old and loved. Just like Maple Bay, this place held onto its past.

"Cory! Jensen!"

We turned toward the sound of Blake's voice and found him and his hunky boyfriend leaning against a black SUV, which was parked in front of a small row of shops. He crossed the street and waved his arms frantically.

Jensen and I waved back and started walking over to him. I was excited about this trip and even more excited that I had become friends with an actual movie star. Blake Hudson was one of the hottest men in Hollywood, and his career had only grown since he came out of the closet. When he invited us to come to Point Pleasant and stay at their cabin for a getaway, I jumped at the chance. I loved a small-town festival, and Blake promised that we would have a blast while we were here. I was also excited to finally meet Danny in person. He and Blake had been together for a couple of years, and we had talked on the phone every now and then, but I had yet to actually meet him.

My eyes bugged out of my head. Blake was a super hot guy with a face and a set of muscles that made people swoon across the world. But Danny... He was in a class all his own. Jensen and Harper were the two most handsome people I think I had ever actually met in real life – until now. Blake's boyfriend was the epitome of Greek perfection.

I heard Jensen chuckle. He knew exactly what I was thinking.

"Yeah... He's so handsome it's actually painful. Yet, I still only have eyes for you." He said lowly, and I grinned like a fool. Tom always knew the right thing to say. It was one of the reasons I was going to marry him.

"How was the ride?" Blake held out his arms as we approached, and I walked right into them and got one of his fantastic bear hugs.

"Terrifying. Jensen tried to kill us."

"Oh, did he?" Blake laughed loudly. "I doubt that. He couldn't bear to live without you. Hey, Tom." I let go of him and took a step back.

"Blake." Jensen came in and gave him a quick hug. Blake patted him on the back. God, they were so butch.

I glanced around Blake and smiled at the approaching figure. "Danny!" I ran over to him, and he literally picked me up and spun me around in another strong embrace. These Point Pleasant boys could hug. It was glorious. "I'm so happy to finally meet you."

"You too, Cory. I feel like we've been friends forever, though, even if we never have met in person." Danny had such a deep velvety voice that it felt like a blanket wrapping over me. But the photos of him did *not* do him justice. I knew he was hot but damn... He was steamy. How could a photo capture the beauty that he radiated? His smile alone made me melt.

"I'm so excited to be here for the festival. I love all that Hallmark shit," I trilled as Danny set me back onto the ground. "The question I have to ask is – why the hell is Blake judging a baking contest? Is he like He-Man Betty Crocker?"

"He burns water when he tries to cook!" Danny cackled, and I knew that we were bound to be new besties. I love a catty remark.

Blake ran his hands through his hair and smirked. "Guilty. They asked, and I said yes. The town is really doubling down on its tourism industry, and I'm the celebrity that couldn't say no."

"It's the only industry we have." Danny grabbed our bag from Jensen and set it down in the back of the truck. "October through March is crazy around here with skiing and winter getaways. Then it picks up again in June through August for the summer. I suppose nine months isn't enough for our mayor. I like the break, honestly."

"Says the man who won't quit being a ski instructor and lifeguard. I tried to make him a house boy." Blake chuckled as he opened the back of his truck and slid our bag inside.

"Bit your tongue. I love it, and what else would I do?" Danny shrugged as he hopped in the back seat and scooted over. "Come on, Cory."

I jumped in and shut the door. Tom sat up front with Blake. I wanted to pinch myself. We had become friends after being trapped in a chalet with a murderer, but it was still surreal. I mean, Blake was a bonafide movie star, and he had invited us to come to join him for the weekend. This was my life, and it was still hard to wrap my head around it.

"You boys want some coffee? I know the perfect place." Blake made a u-turn and headed towards the center of town. "Besides, everyone needs to meet Crystal."

"You're gonna love her." Danny reached over and grabbed my hand like we were besties. "She collects gays. It's her thing, and she is gonna love the two of you."

It didn't take long for Blake to pull into a parking spot. The cutest café stood right in front of us. It looked like something ripped right out of the Hallmark movies I loved. The whole town had that same charm as if it were a movie set and not a place where people actually lived. This was going to be the best weekend ever.

We got out, and Blake opened the door.

"Boys! Do I finally get to meet the two cutest men on the west coast?" A stunning redhead with long flowing locks stood behind the counter. Yep – totally a Hallmark movie, and she was the female lead. She walked around and stood in front of us – sizing Jensen and me up. "Ok, cute doesn't cut it. You two are stunning. Look at all those muscles." She threw her head back and cackled loudly. "I can't wait to hang out and hear all the tea."

"She loves gossip," Danny smirked and walked over to the counter, where he leaned against it.

"I do! I'll close down after lunch. I have Roberta coming in to run the place while the festival's going on. I wanted to spend as much time with you all as possible. I've heard all the stories." She smiled wickedly and elbowed Danny in the ribs. "Since these two lugs didn't introduce me…"

"Please, no introduction is needed with you." Danny laughed happily.

"I'm Crystal, and I've been this one's best friend since Jesus was a baby." She punched Danny in the arm. She was a little violent, and I was living for it.

I was also willing to bet there was one piece of gossip she didn't know. Blake had been given the keys to the secret that we all kept. Victor Sommers, one-time hairdresser and now retiree, was actually a best-selling author of mysteries – Veronica Dean.

"Oh! Let me see the ring." She wiggled her hands in front of her gleefully. I stuck out my hand, and she gay gasped. The diamond sparkled.

"Isn't it gorge?" I glanced over at Jensen, who blushed as he watched me show off the gift that had changed my life forever.

"That is fabulous. Oh, come here." She pulled me into her arms and gave me a big squeeze. Apparently, they were all huggers in this town, and I adored it. "We are going to be new best friends. I expect a text at least twice an hour." She let me go and winked. "I bet you boys need some coffee. How do you take it, gorgeous?" She glanced over at Jensen, who looked befuddled.

"Black, please."

"God, you make my heart melt." She shook her head, and her long strands danced behind her. "Does he have a straight version? Cause I need me one of those." Crystal turned and bounced behind the counter. "Cory? How about you?"

"Uh..."

"How about a vanilla macchiato? You look bougie."

Jensen snorted. He knew I was a CE-Ho.

"That sounds great." I grinned. I mean, it was true. I did like the nicer things in life and had never had a chance to experience them until I met Victor. His secret life had opened doors to a new world for me. I mean, come on! Free cruises, trips to private ski chalets... It wasn't our fault that someone seemed to get murdered wherever we went.

I watched Crystal as she worked her magic. The beans were blended and the milk frothed to perfection before she set it down in front of me. I admit it was a thing of beauty.

"Take a sip and see if that suits you, handsome. I... uh... added a shot of espresso to help get you through the day since the baking contest begins in a few hours."

I almost blew the froth off the milk! "Shit, I can't go looking like this." I knew I should have worn my Marc Jacobs on the trip. It was to die for.

"Oh, honey. Everyone else will be in shorts and tank tops. You have nothing to worry about." Crystal snorted.

"I won't be," Blake sighed heavily. "Don't worry, Cory. We have time to go home and change. I have to be in a suit since it's being televised."

"No! Is it really? Blake, you didn't tell me that! I knew I should have brought my Tom Ford trousers."

"You look good just the way you are." Jensen came up behind me and wrapped his thick arms around my waist – pressing his hard torso against my back. I melted into him.

"Yep. You better tie that shit up quickly. That lug is a catch. You really don't have a brother?" Crystal leaned across the counter and smiled widely.

BLAKE WAS RIGHT.

We did have time to go to the cabin, which was absolutely beautiful. I mean, of course, it was – a movie star lived there. What did I expect?

The cabin set nestled in a small valley between two mountain peaks that still had white caps sitting on top as if it were staged for a film. A small field of wildflowers surrounded the wooden building and made it as picturesque as you could imagine. Like I said, this entire town was ripped out of a Hallmark film and plopped down in this valley just for us. It was as if I had been here before – well, at least in about 45 TV movies.

"Where is this being televised? I have to call everyone I know to watch," I trilled as I paced around their very tastefully decorated cabin in a pair of pants that Victor bought me for my birthday. I had paired it with a light blue silk shirt and my favorite Tom Ford slip-ons. They were so shiny that my image reflected back at me. I looked fabulous and felt like the luckiest bitch in the world as I glanced over at Jensen sipping a bourbon with Danny. They were dressed like gym bros, and my heart stopped and restarted as my eyes raked over their muscles. Yep! I was the luckiest bitch in the world.

"It's being recorded for a future showing on the Gourmet Network. They're paying Blake a fortune to be the host. Honestly, it's ridiculous. Who cares about which home baker makes the best cake?" Danny chuckled as he downed his cocktail. "Would you like something to drink? A martini, maybe?"

"I fucking adore you. Yes, please. A very dry martini where it just glances sideways at the vermouth."

"Got it." Danny stood up and swaggered over to the fully stocked bar.

"I'll have to call the cable company. I don't think we get that channel." I sat down beside Jensen, who pulled me close and kissed me on the head. "Jensen likes to watch football and hunting shows." I rolled my eyes.

"All I watch is sports, and whatever movie Blake forces me to watch." Danny brought my glass over to me, and I carefully took it from his large hands. "I played football in school and grew up on a pair of skis, so…"

"The day I watch sports on TV is the day I check into

rehab," I muttered, and both Danny and Jensen burst into laughter. "But I watch gymnastics. That's a sport."

"And the boys are all quite hot." Jensen grinned.

"I didn't say I didn't like the athletes. A man in a pair of those shoulder things for football makes me weak in the knees." I took a sip and set it down on their table.

"Shoulder pads, and I agree." Danny grinned. "Why do you think I like playing football?"

"Are you all ready?" Blake asked as he descended the stairs straightening his tie.

"Just finishing our drinks. You look very... very sexy in that suit, Hollywood." Danny walked over and grasped Blake's face in his hands before planting a sloppy kiss on his lips.

"If you don't stop that, they'll have to find someone else to host."

"No way! I want that European vacation, so you have to host whether you like it or not." Danny snorted.

"Uh... We can afford a European vacation whenever you..."

"That is not the point. We weren't planning on this, so it's like free or something. Besides, we do have something to plan for, don't we?" Danny's deliberate cadence dripped with implication – you could almost see it.

I smirked and looked between them.

"So, did you choose a date?" I knew they had been talking about it. Blake had inferred about them getting married a few times.

"Talk to Hollywood, over there. With his schedule over the next couple of years, we're going to have to sneak it in." Danny grimaced and looked over at Blake, and smiled. "I'm happy that your film career is going so well. I am, babe. I just wish you would think about eloping and forget the whole idea of inviting everyone we know to celebrate. I really don't need that."

"I'm hoping we can sneak it in between…"

"I'm not sneaking our marriage in between anything. Either we do it and make a plan, or we do it my way and walk into the courthouse alone. You know which one I prefer. But his PR team has other plans, of course."

"This drama is giving me life. Slap him and tell him that a wedding has to be planned a year in advance, and then you, Danny, give him the ultimatum." I cackled. "Seriously, it doesn't really matter, boys. You can get hitched now and then have an elaborate party whenever you want if you want."

"I want the whole big wedding thing." Blake held up his hands to stop any interjections from his hot fiancé. "You know I do. But I'm not against Cory's idea. We could do it now and then plan something for next year up at the lodge. Let's talk about it. I mean, they are here…"

"We could get Crystal and a few of the others to join us. Maybe go have a secret special party here at the house after?" Danny grinned. "What do you think, Cory? Could you maybe help me plan it?"

"Now we're moving really fast." Blake laughed huskily and grabbed his keys. "Let's think about it, and we can discuss it over cocktails tonight. Right now, I have to get us moving. Down 'em, boys, and let's get this shindig on the road."

We did, and it went instantly to my head. I should have eaten first. Gay boy etiquette demands a good lunch before you start downing hard alcohol unless it's at a circuit party. I don't follow directions well. I prefer to dance to my own disco, and the dance floor was a little spinny.

As we pulled up to the court square, which was absolutely fucking adorable, by the way, I noticed a large tent with a camera crew surrounding it. Oh, it was on like Donkey Kong. I glanced at myself in the mirror and made sure my coif was still perfect. I didn't need to worry about it. It was so shellacked that gale force winds would just glide off it.

"Alright, boys, I'll wink at you from the stage," Blake said as we made our way towards the large blue tent. I could see the kitchen set that stood upon the stage with four different stations prepared for the bake-off. This was going to be a blast or really boring. I mean, it was baking – were we really going to sit there while their whatever rose in the oven?

By the look on Danny's face – we were.

"Alright. Love you." Danny kissed Blake's cheek and turned back to us. "You fellas feel like watching dough rise?"

"Is there a bar?" I glanced around.

"It's a bake-off. I'm sure there's cooking sherry." Jensen snuggled up against me and made my heart skip a beat.

"Hey!" Blake called, and we turned to see him standing there waving his arms.

We walked toward him, and as I watched the grin creep across, I became terrified. Was he about to ask if we wanted to be interviewed? I had just flown in, and I knew that I was sporting some serious luggage from getting to the airport so early.

"You want to meet everyone? We have thirty minutes before the contest begins, and I just found out who the judges are. I bet Cory knows all of them." He grabbed me by the hand and pulled me behind the curtains, which kept the audience from the riff-raff.

"Blake, I'm not sure that I should... Shut Up!" I stopped us in our tracks. Standing in front of us were three people I had watched often as I binged cooking competition shows on TV.

"Now he knows how to make an entrance," Gal Kaleery guffawed and slapped the table she was standing in front of.

I was struck dumb. I mean, Blake was a bonafide movie star, but Gal was one of my go-to's whenever I was in a bad mood. Her TV show always made me turn into a couch zombie as I watched the chefs go toe to toe with each other as she threw twist after twist at them. Victor would kick himself for not getting the chance to meet her. He was as much of an addict to the show as I was.

"These are my friends, Cory and Jensen. Fellas, this is Gal Kaleery..."

"I think he knows," Danny put his hand on my shoulder and patted me gently.

"I knew he would. And this is..."

"Holy! Bobbi Day and Alex Topacheffi!" I gasped. It wasn't one of my proudest moments. I was tired, and that made the star-struck stupidity explode out of me the same way I screamed out of the closet, wearing the hinges as earrings.

"It's a pleasure to meet you," Bobbi walked around the table and leaned against it. She was a large lady and wearing heels, so she towered above me.

"How much time do we have?" Alex huffed. "And can someone please get me a cup of coffee? I'm exhausted."

"Alex..." Gal smirked.

"Oh, yeah... It's a pleasure... But I'm serious about the coffee. Where is the damn assistant? I knew coming to a small town, no offense, to do a show like this would be a nightmare. But it's a check, I guess."

"As always, your sunshiny demeanor is a pleasure to be around. You also have a little lipstick there on your cheek."

Bobbi reached across the table and laid her hand on top of his. He pulled it out from under hers and glared before grabbing a napkin and rubbing it off. Yeah, he was just as much of an asshole as he appeared to be on television.

"Did I get it? I guess she didn't notice. My makeup's still good, though, right?" Alex asked haughtily.

"Yes, Alex, you look fine, and you got it off. Would you like to get a selfie with the three of us?" Gal asked sweetly.

I nodded and handed Blake my phone as Jensen, and I arranged ourselves in front of them. I was gobsmacked. I tried to smile and look as hot as I could, which normally was pretty fucking adorable. We'll get back to that photo later, though.

"Hope you enjoy the show, Cory – and keep watching Gal's Games. We have something crazy planned for next season." Gal touched me gently on the arm.

"OK, I'm going to walk them through to meet the contestants. I'll see you all out there." Blake reached over and gently pulled me from the confused and catatonic state I had drifted into. Victor would be so jealous! I couldn't wait to tell him.

"Hope you all enjoy the show," Bobbi said before turning back to the other judges.

"I think Cory is in shock," Jensen took my hand in his and squeezed. We walked out of the holding room and found ourselves backstage. "Come back to me. Life is a lot better when you're witty and catty."

"Even on my death bed, I will be witty and catty." I grinned. I mean, I was on cloud nine. Gal Kaleery was as nice in person as she was on her show. Even when she cut a contestant off, you could feel that she was sorry about having to see them go. She always found something sweet to say to them.

"Blake? Shouldn't you be in makeup?" A deep emotionless voice asked from behind. As one, we all turned.

"Ah, Ry," Blake shrugged and looked over at us. "This is Ry, the director of the bakeoff. This is my fiancé and our friends. Just giving them the VIP tour."

"We don't have much time." Ry stepped down from the platform, and the shadow fell from his handsome and thin face. He was one of the thinnest people I had ever seen. His unkempt blonde hair fell around his face messily. "Nice to meet you all. Please don't make this late, Blake. Time is of the essence. Dealing with Alex is already giving me a bout of angina. Now I can see why his show was canceled."

"Of course," Blake grinned. "Just thought they might want to meet the contestants."

"Oh, God, no!" Another voice made me jump out of my skin – shrill and tense as its painful tone cut through our ears like a whip. "That would be against all the regulations. The FCC could come down on us with hefty fines if you had any contact with the contestants before the show, Blake."

"Oh, I wasn't aware of that, Michael." Blake grimaced. "Sorry. I haven't seen them yet – promise."

"Michael!" Alex bellowed and strode out from behind the curtain. "This is not what I thought it was going to be." He stood there red-faced with his arms crossed.

"No worries, Blake. Rules are rules." Michael glanced over at Alex and turned his back to him.

"I mean, we know them. They are from here, and everyone knows everyone." Danny laughed loudly as he slapped Blake on the shoulder. "Small town and all."

"Oh, is that how it's going to be, Michael?" Alex fumed. Honestly, this was the show I wanted to see.

Michael stiffened and took a deep breath. His heavy frame heaving with annoyance. "Be that as it may. As soon as the contestants arrived, they were sequestered in their own holding area. No contact, OK?" He crossed his arms. Michael, whoever he was, looked like he was overcaffeinated. He even had a little twitch at the corner of his mouth as he stared at us. He had stormy gray eyes and a mustache that you wanted to wax it off. It was so paper thin that he must spend hours grooming it.

"Got it. I'll take them back to the front and go hop in the makeup chair." Blake nodded, and Ry and Michael glanced at each other before turning to the star chef with a bad reputation for throwing fits. Apparently, it was well-earned.

"Michael, I..." Alex began, and Michael held up his hand quickly.

"I don't work for you anymore, Alex. We're here dealing with the show. If you need anything, please talk to the people assigned to deal with your bullshit. It's not my job any longer." Michael laughed coldly. He slapped Ry on the back, and together they went back to where they came from in the shadows behind the set. Alex stood there for a second and stomped back to where he came from.

"Who was that?" Danny whispered. "He really put that asshole in his place, didn't he? Damn..."

"Producer... Come on."

"He's a bit wired." Jensen tsk'ed. I giggled – I had never heard him do that before.

"Most producers are. But he's especially wired." Blake shrugged. "He's been like that every time I've met him."

"Probably coke. I have a coffee addiction, and that was not coffee..." Danny smirked.

"Hmm..." Jensen looked over at me sternly. He was very judgy when it came to drugs. He had a college best friend who became an addict and overdosed when he was a junior. Even the thought of it made him upset. Busting a drug dealer made him very happy, and he was very... very good at it.

Did I mention he was fucking hawt? And we belonged to each other. I loved that. Without him and without me, neither one of us was a fully formed human. I felt it with every glance between us.

Our seats were totally VIP. Danny walked us to the front row – right in the center.

Shit.

That meant we had to stay awake.

2

Abigail Browning was on fire. Not literally... Just buzzing all around her station like the busiest of bees. She shredded some kind of long leaf as if her life depended on it. It wasn't her life that was at stake, but there was a prize of one hundred thousand dollars on the line, and she cooked like she meant business. However, if she was putting grass in her cake, I didn't like her chances.

"In Point Pleasant, that's a shit ton of cash," Danny whispered loudly due to the amount of bourbon he had consumed. "Abigail's a housewife whose husband passed away last year. I don't know if she needs the money or not, but she's acting like she is hungry for a win. She's been in second place at this bake-off for the last five years, and a win would really help her business. She owns a small home business that makes birthday cakes." Danny chuckled. "Yeah, she's hungry for that W."

I agreed. Abigail wanted this win badly.

"The one in the middle is Anne Townsend, and she used to yell at me all the time when I was a kid. She used to be the middle school librarian, and I liked to talk too loudly."

Danny was giving me all the gossip as we watched. Abigail may have been a whirling dervish at her station, but Anne was slow and methodical. I felt like I was watching a chemist at work as she measured and bit her bottom lip before adding anything to her bowl. It was entrancing. "Anne has won the bakeoff for the last nine years, and if she wins today, it would be a decade of trophies for her. My money is on Anne."

Danny glanced over at the entrance to see if he could spot Crystal. She was late, but Danny said that didn't surprise him. Whenever she arrived, according to him, it was right on time in Crystal's world. I admit it made me like her even more. She made a kick-ass coffee, and that was the way to my little overly caffeinated gay heart. With every glance of Danny's, I looked too, hoping to see her vibrant red hair and electric smile.

The other contestant might have been a hundred and ten years old by the looks of her. If a strong breeze had blown into the tent, I would be afraid it might knock her over. The lines on her face were a testament to the years she had probably spent behind a counter making whatever delicious treat she was preparing. I bet she was a great-grandmother who baked every day. She didn't seem to be in a hurry or by the peaceful look on her face, worried in the least as she shredded some carrots.

"Who's the other contestant. She looks so old..." I shrugged as I turned my attention away from Danny and back to the action if that's what you call watching someone mix batter.

"Now that's a fun one. Her name is Veronica Lattice, and she used to be the town's only pharmacist. She retired when I was a freshman. I remember because I got crabs in the locker room and the way she looked at me... Well, I shivered. I'm kind of surprised to see her here. She's pretty reclusive, actually. This is her first year in the bake-off.

"By the looks of it, it might be her last," Jensen giggled. Sorry. They're making me nervous." Jensen whispered loudly. "They all seem way too serious about bread."

I patted his thick thigh gently. "It's like Les Miz, baby. If they don't win, they get thrown in prison for the next decade." I chuckled, proud of my ability to mesh a Broadway classic with what we were witnessing.

"Yeah, I hate that show. All that suffering and regret for toast." He sighed. "I prefer shows like Cats. You don't have to think so hard."

I gay gasped so loudly that people actually turned to stare at me – Danny included. I grimaced and nodded at my etiquette faux pas.

"Jensen's one of my kind of gays, isn't he? Sports and action movies?" Danny grinned, and Jensen actually reached across me to high-five him. I was not impressed. They might be gorgeous, but that's no excuse for liking drivel.

"Did I hear you say the old one gave you crabs?" Jensen grinned stupidly. Jesus, he was so beautiful that it hurt me, and he was all mine. Having someone like him love me the way he did, was a dream I never thought I would have. But here he was.

"That's exactly right. I had a thing for older women..." Danny shook his hair, and his thick dark curls bounced with the effort. "Finally!"

Crystal scooted into her seat. "Sorry. Well, not really. I'm late on purpose and apparently not late enough. They don't even have anything in the oven. Can't they step this up a bit? I don't have a dog n the race this year."

"Our friend, Everett... His mom Sandra usually enters

the bake-off, but when she found out it was being televised, she dropped out, and that's how Veronica got her place. We always came because we love Sandra. She's the best." Danny explained.

"Danny also used to fuck her son." Crystal cackled.

"Now we're talking. Give me the gossip." Finally, something exciting to talk about.

"They dated for a while and..."

"It didn't work out, but I was the best man at his wedding. Which I also planned. Blake is Everett's husband's brother..."

"Isn't it so incestuous? Danny has fucked Everett- Oh! Everett's husband's name is Evan. Isn't it confusing? They're both Evs... weird and confusing when you're around them, and Everett has been one of our besties since we all met. Anyway... Danny has fucked Evan's husband and his brother." Crystal stuck her tongue out at her best friend.

I almost applauded! "Scandalous. Give me more!"

"Danny and Everett were a hot, humid mess."

"Why are we friends?" Danny chuckled.

"Oh, Danny..."

"It looks like Abigail is making a move. She's leaving her station." Jensen pointed.

"She's walking, Jensen. Maybe she forgot eggs?" I giggled. I was in my element and surprised by how much fun the bake-off actually was.

"No. She's buzzing right by the kitchen and..."

"Maybe she's going to off the competition. Slam the old woman over the head with that rolling pin she's clutching," I said gleefully. "Wait... Why does she have a rolling pin? Aren't they making cakes?"

We all turned to watch – caught up in the... Well, action,

I guess, as we waited for Abigail to bring down the pin over little frail Veronica's head.

"You'd think Anne would be the one she wanted to take out since she always wins," Danny said conspiratorially, getting caught up in my fun.

"Y'all are gonna feel like shit if she does kill poor old Veronica. It would serve her right. Veronica's a bitch." Crystal reached over and grabbed my hand. I felt like I belonged here with my new friends. I just wish Victor could have been here, too. These were the kind of games that we would play. The kind of gossip we would share.

"Can I please get some of the cream of tartar, please?" Abigail said slowly and firmly as she stood a few feet away from Veronica's station. The older woman gave her a long glance. She just stood there like a statue as she sized Abigail up. I mean, come on, this is a small town, and I'm sure they knew each other. Apparently, they didn't like each other very much. Abigail clenched the rolling pin so hard you could see the whites of her knuckles.

"I don't have it." She replied icily as she turned back to her station and picked up a carrot.

"It's there on the edge." Abigail pointed with the pin.

"Huh... I didn't see it there." Veronica shrugged as she raked the carrot across the shredder thing she was using. Sorry, I don't bake. I order a mean pizza, though.

"Can I please have it?" Abigail said again – her voice raising.

"Oh, that's right... You can't come into my station." Veronica snickered as she walked over to the edge and slowly picked up the small jar. "Must be weird having to follow the rules, huh? You were never very good at that."

"Ms. Lattice..." Abigail sighed and held out her hand. "Please?"

"Not used to saying that either, and I think I've heard three of them now." Veronica slowly moved the spice jar towards her, and I thought she might pull it back away in a truly psych moment. But she didn't. She gave it to her, and Abigail turned and mumbled under her breath before arriving back at her station.

"I think I know what Abigail called her." Crystal guffawed. Throwing her head back and letting her loud cackle flow uninhibitedly.

"Yeah, that was better than an episode of Law and Order." Jensen rolled his eyes. "Tense, though. I thought I might have to arrest her for homicide the way she was brandishing that wooden club."

"That's called a rolling pin, honey." I put my hand behind his neck and ran my fingers through the short hair on his nape. I could do that all day. "My big butch homo."

"My God, I am in love with you two."

A man behind us shushed us loudly, and Danny scooted down in his seat, trying to suppress his giggle. Crystal just turned and gave him a look. You know the one... It was powerful, and the man didn't say anything again. I guess he got the point.

We watched.

Abigail put her shredded leaves in a food processor and blended.

Veronica started adding her carrots to a blender.

Anne was as cool as a cucumber and was already mixing her batter as she leaned against the counter.

It was not riveting. But I was in it. I would see who the victor would be, no matter how badly I wanted to take a nap. Would people notice if I just shut my eyes for a quick second? Duh! It was being televised, and what if, at that moment, the camera cut to the very good-looking group right up front. Victor would never let me live that down.

Viciousness towards your best friend is in the gay DNA.

"And it looks like our nine-time Point Pleasant champion will be the first to get her batter in the oven. What are you making, Anne?" Blake leaned over the side of her station and beamed his trademark million-dollar smile towards the camera.

"Baumkuchen?" Anne looked up and noticed the camera moving towards her. She bit her bottom lip.

"Baum... what?" Blake chuckled deeply, and the rest of us burst into laughter at the stupid look on his face. He was doing very well, and if his movie career ever tanked, he would be a good host on one of those HGTV shows.

"Baumkuchen. It's one of the hardest cakes to make in the world. It's also called a tree cake because of all of the layers that look like rings on a log. I like to call this one my tree of life cake. You pour one ring at a time into the pan and bake each ring separately to achieve the delicate layers."

"Am I bothering you? Do you need to get back to work?"

"I do, Blake. This cake won't work if I'm not exceedingly careful. It's bake, pour, bake, pour and try to get the icing done on time, too."

"I'll let you get back to it then. Do you think you have enough time to..."

"Baking is science, Blake, and I can do this. I just can't have any mistakes."

"Alright... Has anyone in the audience ever heard of Baumkitchen?" He shrugged, and a few people raised their hands. Crystal included.

"It's Baumkuchen, hot stuff." Crystal cackled, and Blake smirked. "It's a German cake and absolutely divine if it's done right. In Germany, they actually cook this cake on a spit instead of an oven."

"A spit?" Blake shook his head as if the idea blew his mind.

"Don't ask. I have no idea." Crystal grinned, and Blake patted Anne's station and moved over to Abigail's.

"And what tasty treat do you have in store for us, Abigail? I saw you ripping up some kind of leaf over here. I thought that's a little odd to put something green in a cake, but..."

"I'm making my world-famous Pandan Chiffon Cake. It's a recipe that my grandmother brought over with her when she came to this country. It's going to blow your mind, and hopefully the judges."

"I've never heard of Pandan."

Abigail turned on her mixer and took a step toward Blake. "It's an amazing plant grown only horticulturally. There are no wild Pandan plants in existence, as far as I know. It's used for all kinds of things, Blake. Cooking, medicine, and perfume are just a few of its uses. It is one of the components of jasmine rice, and its flavor can vary as to how you cook it. It can be floral, sweet, grassy, or even sometimes taste like vanilla. All depends on the use you put it to."

"I feel like I just took a science class." He smirked out at the audience.

Abigail took a small spoon of her greenish mixture and held it up his nose. "Can you smell that?"

He inhaled and opened his eyes widely. "That's... Wow, that smells amazing."

"See? It's a staple in my house, and hopefully, people will learn a little more about it. I'm really tired of having to special order it. These leaves here came out of my greenhouse, but normally I buy it from a West Coast market and have it shipped here."

"The things you learn on a baking show. Has anyone in the audience ever heard of the pandan cake?" No one raised their hands. "Then it's a first for everyone. I wish you could all smell what I just did."

"My dough looks perfect. Now I have to get this into the pans." Abigail unlocked her mixer and pulled out the bowl. "I'm coming for you, Anne." She teased.

"Hope you enjoy that second place spot, Abs, because that's where you're staying," Anne smirked as she opened the oven and took out a pan before inspecting it carefully.

"The trash talk is real, folks." Blake chuckled and walked over to Veronica. "And what are you making for us, Ms. Lattice?"

"My famous carrot cake. It's an old family recipe, so don't ask. I don't want to have to kill you." She said so steelily that it made me sit up straight, and I wasn't anywhere as close to her as Blake was. He just grinned and stared at her.

"Well, I would hate that too. Death does not become me."

"The trick is not to let the other people bother you. I've always thought baking was for the loners, and all the chat around here makes me miss my own kitchen." She took the spatula out of the bowl and watched the batter run down it. "Now, if you don't mind, I need to pour this and get it in the oven."

"No worries. I would hate to get in the way." Blake backed up and smirked at the audience. Everyone giggled, and Veronica Lattice stared up at everyone with a glare so cold that the laughter trailed off quickly. "You really are killing me up here, Ms. Lattice."

She mumbled something under her breath, and Danny chuckled quietly.

"She really is a piece of work," Danny muttered.

"Now that we've met the contestants and seen what they are baking, we're going to head to our next commercial break. Who will win? Will it be the home baker with her own birthday cake business, the retired librarian who is a nine-time champ, or the retired pharmacist who just threatened my life? Stay tuned and keep watching The Great Small Town Bakeoff!

"Well, that was something!" Blake smiled. "We're taking a quick break as the bakers keep working. You'll notice that the cameras are still filming, so we don't miss anything exciting that might happen." Blake handed the microphone over to an assistant.

"Like there's a snowball chance in hell of that," Crystal muttered.

"I'm going back to make up for a bit, and we'll be back with the commentating in about ten minutes."

He walked off, and his shoulders slumped – happy to be off the stage.

"I guess all baking shows are this boring. I mean, it's mixing, stirring, baking, and decorating. But they make them look much more exciting on TV." Danny hunkered down in his seat. "Crystal, did you bring in the giggle juice?"

She pulled four water bottles out of her handbag and handed them around. "It's just vodka and seven, so it will look like water. Trust me, this is how Danny and I get through this every year. Usually, we have more of an entourage with us, but since Everett's mom isn't participating... It's just us here for Blake. The things a girl does for one of her besties with testes," Crystal laughed and smacked

Danny on the cheek. "And from the gossip I've heard, most of them are very well..."

"Crystal!" Danny blushed.

"She was going to say endowed," I giggled to Jensen. My hand slipped over his thigh. "If she only knew..."

"You know I heard that, don't you. He looks like he's packing a..."

"Crystal, these are fucking insane!" Danny gasped as he took a sip.

"Yeah, I couldn't remember how many shots we put in, so they may be lethal." She cackled and glanced behind her to stare at the man who had shushed her earlier. I was in love with her. She was a badass who took no shit, and that was exactly how I liked my women.

Blake came back.

We sipped our drinks.

They made frosting.

We sipped our drinks.

Cakes came out of the oven, and in the case of Anne's German Baumkuchen, it came out of the oven every three to four minutes. I was fascinated as I watched her... Well, maybe fascinated is too strong of a word, but I was in it, and interested. She pulled the cake out and added another layer of batter on top like she was a machine.

Abigail seemed to have trouble with her frosting. She threw the first batch out and started again. A twisted look of anger stayed plastered on her face as she cracked eggs in a flurry.

Veronica, on the other hand, looked like she was bored. Her frosting was finished, and now she was rolling something out at her station – decorations, I assumed. I mean, it was a carrot cake – I bet it was some kind of carrot.

"Is anyone else hot?" Crystal asked loudly – standing up

and unbuttoning her shirt. She glanced down and noticed the look of horror on my face. "Relax. I have a t-shirt on."

"It's hot. But I think you have the vodka sweats." Danny pointed to her empty bottle.

"Oh, my God! I drank the whole thing." Crystal cackled.

Danny held up his empty bottle, too. Crystal laughed louder. Abigail stared out at her with a look of pure annoyance. I sunk into my seat and gripped Jensen's leg. He took my hand in his and held it tightly.

"There are only thirty minutes left in the competition, and the cakes are still in the oven. Now, I am not a baker, but what happens when you put icing on a hot cake? They need to get them out quickly and put them in the cooler." Blake strode out center stage. "Ladies? Are you close."

Abigail opened the oven and tested her cake. Pulling it out of the oven and walking it quickly over to the cooler where it would cool down. I had seen contestants do this on many baking competition shows.

Anne poured one last ring of batter and stuck it back in the oven before running back to her station. She started cracking eggs and adding sugar before running back to the oven and pulling her pan out. It was a large pan, and it took her both hands to carry it as she made her way to her own cooler.

Veronica checked her watch and stayed behind the counter.

"Veronica? Is your cake close to being done?" Blake asked, and she shrugged.

"It's ready when I say it is. It'll be done on time, so stop having a hissy, Blake." She said dryly.

Blake laughed loudly and looked out at the audience, who snickered. "Veronica Lattice, everyone. She's here all evening."

He went back to his stool, and a few minutes later, Veronica stood up and took her cake out of the oven, and placed it slowly in the cooler.

It felt like time slowed down – then sped up – then slowed back down.

I was getting bored but tried to be as engaged as possible just in case the camera decided to sneak a shot of me. What would my friends say if the camera caught me with my mouth agape in boredom? They'd never let me live it down and start creating memes. I worried way too much about what other people thought and always had. Before meeting Victor, I was a scared twinky mess most of the time. It was his friendship and guidance that made me blossom into the semi-strong person I now was.

But like all gay people – we could be vicious to one another. I saw something posted on Instagram the other day that said when a gay person called you bitch, you were probably friends. If they called you sweetie – sworn enemies. I couldn't afford to be a meme. What if I went viral?

Seriously, watching people make icing or whatever they were doing was lulling me into a stupor. I pinched my thigh and forced myself to sit up as straight as possible. Jensen slid his arm behind me and rolled his eyes. He, too, was having a hell of a time staying alert.

Finally, one after another, the ladies went to the cooler to retrieve their cakes. Veronica frowned as she pulled hers out, and that meant her cake was still warm. At least, that's what I assumed. Anne and Abigail grinned widely as they carefully carried their pans to the station.

"We are down to the last fifteen minutes of the competition, ladies and gentlemen." Blake stayed seated and watched from the edge of the stage as the ladies started icing and decorating their cakes in a hurry.

"Normally, they are further ahead than this," Danny shrugged and crossed his arms.

"If they all look like shit, then they're all in the same boat. The mayor will be pissed, though. He worked hard to get this on TV. If The Pleasant puts up fucktastic cakes, he'll see it as a major issue."

"Blake said it's only a thirty-minute show. The drama will come in the editing. It always does."

"Someone will have to die to make this watchable. Jesus." Crystal huffed and hung her head back over her chair with a look of torture on her face.

Jensen chuckled. "Well... We're here, so it's a strong possibility," he muttered in my ear.

"Stop that. Let's not put that out into the world. I need a break from murder and mayhem." I grinned. "Besides, no one ever gets murdered in a Hallmark movie. It's against the trope."

"In a small town, just like in ours, there's always secrets and bad things happening. Most small towns are just very good at hiding them."

Before I could respond, Blake jumped up from his stool and walked over to the contestants. "That's beautiful, Abigail. What kind of frosting is that."

"It's my own special recipe for a very delicate chiffon icing with just a hint of Pandam in it. You don't want the frosting to overpower the cake."

"So, you won't give us the recipe?"

"No way, Blake. This will go to my grave with me."

"And what are you using Anne for your... I won't even try to pronounce it cake?"

"Just like Abigail, I have a secret recipe for a frosting that I only use on this cake. The layers are so delicate that not any frosting will do. It's almost a glaze that holds its shape, so I can make this cake look exactly like a log."

"Fascinating. I had no idea there could be so many kinds of icing."

"That's because you probably have never baked a cake." Veronica snickered, and the audience roared. Even if her cake was total shit – the audience adored her sour exterior. She was quite funny in a dry and sarcastic way.

"That is not true. I made cupcakes when I was in middle school. Mom had to call the fire department to tell them the house wasn't on fire." Blake mugged out to the audience. "And... I still ate the crispy basta... uh... cupcakes." He blushed. "How's your decorating coming, Veronica?"

"Like a one-legged dog running after a ball. The cake was still warm, so the icing is runny. I have to get it on quick with the decorations and put it back in the freezer until it's time to serve the damn thing."

"And language." Blake chuckled. "You have five minutes."

"It is what it is... "

A person ran over to Blake and whispered in his ear. He nodded.

"Veronica, so you know, you're cake has to be out of the freezer and on the stand at the end of time."

"Then I guess it's not going into the freezer, is it, hotshot?" She took her spatula off the cake and started putting on the toppings. Even from where I was, I could see the icing starting to slide. "Stupid rules..." She continued mumbling under her breath, and I was sure that the sound guys were having a riot listening to her.

"This is a blind-tasting, ladies and gentlemen. After the cakes are on their stands, our judges will be introduced, and the contestants will be in seclusion backstage while the judges sample and rate their hard work. Does anyone else feel like this is an algebra test? I was told by one of the judges backstage that baking is a lot like chemistry. I guess we'll see which of these hard-working contestants will get an A and which will have to take the class again because of a failing grade. One-minute contestants. Get those cakes on the stand!"

Everyone sat up, knowing that the real show was about to begin.

Anne was first as she transferred her cake to the stand. Veronica, who had decided to give up, I guess – slid her cake onto the stand and sat down with a deep frown for all to see. Abigail looked like she was about to drop her cake as she made the transfer, but she quickly steadied herself and carefully placed it on the glass stand before taking a step back.

"And time. Let's have a big round of applause for our contestants as they make their way backstage for the judging." Blake grinned.

The contestants all made their way backstage, with Veronica bringing up the rear and glancing back over her shoulder to stare at us. Maybe she was embarrassed that her cake looked like an orange mud pit sloping in on itself, or maybe she just wanted to scare us into not making fun of her. She was quite intimidating for an old woman. I bet in her youth, she was all spitfire and venom. Really, I guess not much had changed for her except for the wrinkles that now lined her face.

I didn't know her, but she reminded me of a few older ladies from my hometown of Maple Bay. Veronica seemed to be just as salty as Betty Davis, who owned and was the voice of The Maple Bay radio station. She was a piece of work, but I admired the shit out of her. No one took advantage of Betty, and I would wager the same for Veronica.

"Let me introduce you to our panel of celebrity judges. First off is the lady who taught cooks across the country how to get the most out of their pantry. From Bobbi's Pantry – Bobbi Day." The audience all clapped loudly. Bobbi had been a staple on most food channels for a long time. She sauntered out and waved happily before taking her seat.

"Our next judge likes to take you around the world with his cuisine, and his show, The Topacheffi Effect, has won numerous Emmy Awards in the reality competition. Ladies and gentlemen, Alex Topacheffi." The crowd clapped happily, but the sound was nowhere as loud as it had been for Bobbi. Alex was known for throwing tantrums and making people cry on his shows. Being mean may make you famous but not universally adored. He walked out and quickly raised his hand in the air, but his face told everyone that he didn't really want to be here. It was a paycheck and nothing more – just as he said. He looked around and undid the top button on his shirt, and pulled the collar away from his neck.

"Last – but not least... Who here likes to play games? Leading our judging panel is the world-renowned chef with a penchant for causing chaos with a smile. Ladies and gentlemen, the gal with the highest ratings in daytime, Gal Kaleery!" The audience stood on their feet and screamed as they applauded. Everyone loved Gal. She bowed and blew kisses as she made her way to the center of the judging table, where she almost fell over but steadied herself on the edge of it.

"Well, that's a warm welcome. Small towns always know how to make you feel right at home, and I bet these bakers are going to blow us all away. Am I right, Point Pleasant?" Gal sat down and nodded to the other two. The crowd cheered. "We are looking for the yummy factor. A dessert that makes you want to take another bite and then maybe another slice. We're also judging on the decorations." She glanced at the cakes and giggled. "Nothing too fancy, I see up there. But I bet they taste delicious."

A different assistant went to each cake and brought it to the judging table. They pointed at the cakes, and Alex scoffed when they all turned to the carrot cake. The assistants sliced each cake for the judges to taste. The crowd quieted down as the first dessert was placed in front of the judges.

"The first piece of culinary delights they sat before us is the carrot cake. It's still quite warm, and the icing has melted and become a rather unpleasant looking consistency." Gal stared at it. "But it does smell quite delicious."

"It's dense in the perfect way a carrot cake should be. It's moist and fluffy, and you can see all the little bits of carrot cooked into the batter. It looks quite lovely." Bobbi took her fork and poked at it.

"It surprisingly tastes much better than it looks. You can't ice a warm cake and expect it to go well. I'd fire my pastry chef if I had to serve this, but I will admit, it tastes quite pleasant." Alex sat his fork down with a clunk against the china and sat back. He covered his mouth and coughed, wiping his mouth with a napkin. "Excuse me."

"I'll agree with you on the taste. This baker knows what they're doing in the kitchen. I'm going to assume time got away from them." Gal nodded. "It's good enough that I had a second bite. The frosting does have a bit of an aftertaste, though."

"That can happen when the cake is frosted too soon. The heat starts breaking the icing apart. It's a delicate thing that can be destroyed quickly." Bobbi answered, and she and Gal both set their forks down and waited for the next slice to be brought to them. The assistants placed the tree cake in front of them.

"Wow, is all I can say!" Gal enthused. "This cake had the best decoration, and I wondered if it might be... And it is. How badass do you have to be to make a Baumkuchen in a competition with a time limit?"

"Agreed. Even I am impressed at someone attempting this. It's quite difficult, and only truly advanced bakers could pull this off." Alex said smugly as he stretched his neck to the side as if he were trying to pop it back into place. "I once made one on a spit the way it's supposed to be made, and I can tell you it didn't turn out very well for me."

"I watched that episode. It was one of the best comedies I've ever seen." Bobbi laughed loudly and slapped the table. "I thought I might bust a rib."

"Watching a master fail is riveting television." Gal chuckled.

"I hate you both." Alex grinned, and I couldn't tell if he was playing or not.

"No, you don't. Without us, you'd have no one." Bobbi said coyly. "Let's taste it. It does look quite amazing."

"You can see each ring of the process. I'm quite impressed with this cake." Alex nodded. "It was also quite pretty from the outside. It looks like a tree stump. Very well decorated. Whoever made this has a very steady hand." He coughed again. "Goodness! Excuse me again, everyone."

"It's not dry, which Baumkuchen can be because of all the time the bottom layers spend in the oven. It has the perfect texture and consistency." Bobbi cut into the slice and moaned as she put it in her mouth. "Brandy! She put Brandy in it. Perfect."

"Agreed. It is scrumptious. The icing is not too sweet but sweet enough and pairs excellently with the light brandy flavor of the cake. Marvelous." Gal shook her head. "I'm flabbergasted as to how this cake happened on this stage."

"Yeah, this is top-notch. This is a cake that is hard to beat." Alex took another bite, and Gal almost fell out of her chair.

"A second bite. That's high praise coming from you, Alex."

"Alright... Let's try this next cake. I'm intrigued." Alex took another quick bite of the Baumkuchen before scooting the plate away.

"Lastly, we have the Pandan Chiffon Cake. Such a strange dessert to find in this area of the country." Gal said bemusedly as she cut it with her fork.

"That's... fairly brilliant! When you cut into it, you can feel how soft and pillowy it is. The fragrance just... hits you in all the right ways." Bobbi sniffed the cake and poked at it with her fork.

Alex cut into the cake and took a bite. "It has all the right things happening for it." He reached down and placed his hand on his heart, and took a deep breath. "This... uh... baker must have used fresh Pandam... and..." Alex stopped, and his fork fell from his hand. He reached up and put his hands around his neck.

"Alex?" Gal asked quickly.

Alex gasped and fell face-first into his cake. He didn't move again.

Bobbi screamed.

3

So, the evening had a surprise. The crowd went crazy as the ambulance was called, and the audience was ushered out. We waited on the street for two hours and were very thankful to Crystal for the cocktails. Blake was being held back with the rest of the production staff, contestants, and judges, while everyone else in the audience had left. We waited. It was more boring than watching a cake bake.

Blake finally walked out with a few of the others that were not allowed to leave. He looked grim and incredibly unhappy.

"Alex passed away." He stopped in front of us, and I noticed that the color had drained completely from his face. "They held us back and have put the place on lockdown. No one is allowed to leave The Pleasant for now."

"Did he have a heart attack?" Crystal asked and looked as if she would rather be anywhere else in the world but here.

"They don't think so. He was foaming at the mouth and couldn't breathe. He had all the signs of asphyxiation." Blake was shook, honey! He was on the verge of losing it.

"Can we leave?" Danny reached over and pulled his fiancé to him, taking him in a strong embrace. Blake nodded.

"Maybe we should go back to your house?" Crystal suggested, and we all got into Blake's truck with Danny behind the wheel and Crystal followed behind.

"Foaming at the mouth?" Jensen said quietly. "That doesn't sound natural. Not even anaphylaxis would cause someone to start doing that, so it couldn't have been an allergic reaction."

I just sat there for a second and clenched my fist. This was my fucking vacation – my getaway – and here we were with another fucking dead body. "Am I cursed?"

"You sound like Victor?" Jensen pulled me against him and wrapped his arm around me.

"Maybe it's not Victor? Maybe it's me?" I was a young gay man who was more than moderately attractive. I thought the world revolved around me.

"Don't be stupid." Jensen bent down and kissed the top of my head. "Shit happens. It just so happens when we're here. But that doesn't mean we have to do anything, Cory. This town has a police department that will deal with it. Tomorrow we can wake up and enjoy what's left, ok?"

I nodded, but I knew my life was nothing short of a lifetime movie drama where everyone wanted to kill me. It had been that way for far too long.

We pulled up to Blake's, and all got out of our cars. We went inside, and Danny started making cocktails while Blake changed out of his television clothes.

"So, who won?" Crystal said suddenly.

"I guess no one did. The judges never had a chance to say." Danny shook his cocktail shaker and poured a frothy mixture into a crystal martini glass. I think we were all feeling way too sober after a death happened in front of us.

"Dude! It was the person who made that cake that no one could pronounce. Blamkoosen or something." Jensen sat down on the couch as Danny brought him over a pink cocktail. At least it would match my outfit.

"I don't know. That Pandam cake was getting a lot of likes, too," I suggested.

"He died after eating a bite of it." Crystal huffed. "You can't come back from that."

"If Vicki were here, she would figure it out. It might as well be from one of her mysteries." I shrugged. "I'm really tired of people dying when I go on vacation."

"People die on vacations a lot." Danny shrugged as he handed me a drink.

"Trust me, I know." I sighed heavily.

"I guess your sheriff is used to dealing with this kind of thing." Jensen took a sip and set his glass down on the table.

"Oh, I'm sure he's not. I mean, we get a drowning every now and then or a skier who runs into a tree, but nothing like this. He's probably shitting himself right now." Crystal laughed. "Sorry, too soon?"

"Yeah, we don't really have murders and shit like that here. The last time there was a crime anywhere as bad as this, if this was a crime, was when little Markie Pranston killed his parents with a butcher knife." Danny sat down and offered Crystal her cocktail. He put what I assumed would be Blake's down on the table in front of him as we waited for him to come back down.

"Holy shit! I forgot all about Markie fucking Pranston. He was such an asshole." Crystal shivered.

"Yeah, he came back from trick or treating and had eaten way too much candy. He grabbed the butcher knife and stabbed his father in the chest. Then went upstairs and slit his mother's throat while she was sleeping. He was a year ahead of us in school. We were in, like, third grade or something at the time."

"Was that really the last murder that we've had? I guess it was." Crystal looked deep in thought.

"Holy shit. That's really intense. Like Michael Meyers or Freddie type of shit!" Jensen scrunched his face up as he took it all in.

"Kind of. That was, like, over twenty years ago. I guess he's still in some kind of warped mental hospital or prison. God, I don't know. Maybe he's been released by now. I mean, he was like nine or something." Crystal shrugged. "Danny? Can I have another? I gulped this shit down."

"Hey." Blake descended the stairs and stared at Danny's frothy cocktail. "Love you. But I'm doing a bourbon neat after the day I've had." He walked over and poured himself a large amount and dropped an ice cube in it.

"I don't blame you." Jensen chuckled.

"I meant to tell you that I..." the doorbell rang. "Well, I guess you'll find out now." Blake walked over to the front door and nodded at whoever was on the other side.

A police officer walked into the room.

"Sorry about this." He took off his hat and stood there with it in his hands. He was maybe fifty and looked about as sweet as they come. He looked nervous, and he took his free hand and ran it through the few strands he had left on top of his head. "I'm just a... Well, it's nice to meet you, I guess – even if it's... Well..."

I smiled. I couldn't help myself. He was the epitome of the fumbling older sheriff in a small town. He fidgeted as he stood there, and I had to stop the giggle that threatened to erupt. He was pulled right out of the stock characters that appeared in Hallmark films, just like the rest of this adorable town.

Then it hit me.

Why is the sheriff here?

"Sheriff Roy, how can we help you?" Danny looked at his fiancé with wide eyes.

"Well, Blake here mentioned to me in his interview that you all had guests in town from Maple Bay. He... uh... told me about you guys, and... Well, I googled you, and I have to tell you, fellas, I am way out of my league here." He rocked back and forth on his feet, and I was starting to get seasick watching him.

"Are you looking for some advice, Sheriff?" Jensen asked, leaning back on the couch. His body tightened against mine.

"Well, you could say that. Are you Tom Jensen?"

"Sheriff? Please sit down." Blake offered the chair that he was standing next to. Sheriff Roy moved over and sat down, placing his brown hat on top of his lap.

"Yes, sir. Deputy Jensen at your service."

"That means you must be Cory. You've helped solve quite a few cases with Ms. Dean, I've seen."

"Well, I've... been a help, I guess," I said nervously. I understood why he was here, and I wasn't exactly pleased about it. It was my fucking vacation.

"That's just fine, and I'm happy you're here. I'm a little in over my head here, boys. The last crime we had in The Pleasant was a stolen bicycle. I mean, we get some drunk and disorderly tourists that spend a night in jail to sleep it off, but Point Pleasant is one of the safest small towns in America. I have two deputies, and one of them joined the force a couple years ago when old man Sweets retired, and he's greener than a Granny smith. The other gets confused when they write a speeding ticket. We're not exactly equipped to deal with a murder."

"A murder? You're sure that he was killed, and it wasn't..."

"Well, toxicology is being run at the hospital right now, and once the autopsy is done, we will know for sure. But looking at the way it happened – I mean, he's a celebrity... Everyone in the audience saw him foaming at the mouth and having what looked like a seizure. According to his manager, he had never experienced anything like that before. My little niece, she has seizures every now and then, and they don't look anything like that."

"So, you're assuming that he was poisoned somehow?"

"If it looks like a duck..."

"Have you locked down the crime scene?" Jensen ran his hand through his hair, and I knew that we weren't going to say no. His jaw had that firm set he got whenever he was working.

"I have a deputy there, and we are gathering and boxing everything by station and dressing area. I thought that would be the best way to handle it since there are not really any walls to speak of. Besides, the tent will need to come down in a couple days, or the city will have to pay extra."

"What exactly are you asking of us, Sheriff?" Jensen sat forward, his shoulders clenched tightly.

"Well, would you fellas like to be hired as consultants for the case? I can't really deputize that young man, but I could you since you're already a badge. But consultants can be... uh... non-badge." He wrang his hat and then straightened the brim back out. "Sorry, I'm a little caught off guard by all of this. We're not used to having to deal with the kind of PR that his death might bring."

"You have to understand, we're on vacation and..."

"Oh, I understand. If you can't..."

"How can we say no, Sheriff? A man's dead, and if it was foul play, we have a duty to help since you asked." I said quickly, wishing I didn't feel so strongly about it. "Right, Jensen?"

"I agree. Are you sure you're alright with helping out, babe? I can help while you get some well-deserved r and r."

"I'd rather be with you. Besides, you might need me."

"There's no one else I'd rather solve a murder with." He winked, and I could feel the blush creep across my skin.

"It's settled then. What I was going to say, Sheriff, is we're only here for a few days, and I don't see how we can extend our visit since we both have jobs that are expecting us back home. But while we're here, we'll do what we can."

"Great! What do you want to do first?"

"I think we need to see what evidence you've collected."

"And first thing tomorrow, we need to go back to the venue. Please keep an officer posted there so no one can come back inside, even if you have packed away the evidence." Jensen stood up and stretched – his shirt riding up and showing a little of his tanned skin beneath. "I have to ask. They did wear gloves and bagged everything, correct?"

Sheriff Roy nodded. "They may be green, but they know enough to do that."

"We'll see you in the morning then, Sheriff. Can you have copies of the notes you took today when everyone was questioned to give us? We'll probably have some follow-ups, but that would be a good place to start."

"Of course. I can't thank you both enough. I'll have everything for you and will see you in the morning. Eight works for you?"

We nodded, and I instantly regretted it. I was exhausted and wouldn't be able to go to sleep easily tonight.

"I'll see you then. Thanks fellas." Sheriff Roy turned and without another word, walked out through the door.

"I should have warned you, but I didn't know he was going to... do this." Blake frowned. "Sorry about your getaway. You know you're welcome to come whenever you want, but after this vacation, you might not want to ever come again."

"You're so dramatic." I chuckled. "Trust me, by this point, we're used to it. I just wish we could get Vicki and Harper to join us, but they're away too."

"It's just us, then." Jensen bent down and kissed the top of my head. "We're going to be fine."

"Well, we have 72 hours left to crack the case. If we can't solve it by then, leaving this unfinished will kill me."

"Then let's solve it. All we need is a little luck."

"Oh, you'll find plenty of that in The Pleasant," Danny said pluckily.

"Alex sure didn't," Blake said, and for a few moments, no one said anything.

The truth was the truth.

4

Danny pulled up to the large park, and we saw the sheriff standing by his range rover. He looked like he hadn't slept very well last night, either. I barely had a disco nap.

"Just call me when you're ready for me to pick you up. Tonight, if you have time, Blake and I thought we might go out for a drink or two with some friends." Danny looked at us, hopefully.

"Sounds good, I think. We'll have to see where the day takes us." Jensen shrugged.

"Good. Just call me. I'd say have fun, but... I guess I don't know what to say. Good luck?" Danny looked at us remorsefully. He knew how bad I had wanted this vacation.

"Thanks. Talk to you later." We opened and doors and got out. Danny pulled away, and we walked to meet the waiting sheriff.

"Nervous?" Jensen took my hand in his.

"Would it be weird if I said no?" I bit my bottom lip. Death had become all too familiar to me, and I didn't like that, but I didn't *not* like it, either. I didn't miss the boy I used to be who was scared all the time. Meeting and becoming Victor's best friend had changed me for the better. Now, I strode into the room where the killer might be hiding as I tried to find them. I didn't say I had gotten any smarter.

"Thanks for meeting me." Sheriff Roy looked just as nervous today as he did last night. He glanced up at the sky and then burst into a smile. "It's gonna be another pleasant day in The Pleasant."

"Someone was stationed here all night, Sheriff?" Jensen went right to business. It was hot.

"Yes, MacLeery was here all night, and he said it was quiet." The sheriff pointed to a patrol car sitting over at the edge of the large tent. "He patrolled hourly to keep an eye on things."

"Good. Can we start in the judges holding room? I assume that's where they got ready?" Jensen pulled out a small notepad.

"I... uh... I'm not sure of that. We'll have to ask someone who was involved with the production." Sheriff Roy looked at us perplexed. "Is that important?"

"I don't think we know yet." I shrugged. "Everything is important until it isn't."

"Oh, I see..." He took his hat off and gave it a good squeeze. Seriously, how that brim was still holding up was beyond me.

"Is there someone from the production that can come and meet us, Sheriff?"

"Please, call me Roy. We're both lawmen, and I've only been the sheriff for a few years. Still feels a little odd to me." He grinned as if he didn't have a care in the world. I guess he didn't. He had us working the case for him.

"Can you make that call, Roy?" Jensen stopped in his tracks and crossed his arms.

"Oh, of course. Hold on a second. You fellas can feel free to go inside and look around all you want. I'll have to get the info from MacLeery." Sheriff Roy waved at us and turned to walk over to the setting patrol car.

"This is not going to be easy. He's too nice. It makes me uncomfortable." Jensen sighed. "My first partner on the force was a lot like him – easy going and way too trusting. He almost got me shot in the back."

"You never really talk about your time before Maple Bay and working for Harper."

"Yeah... I guess I don't. It wasn't all bad, but when you're in a large city, the things you see keep you up at night."

"Has Maple Bay been that much better? I mean, there was a stiletto in someone's brain."

"Murder is what it is. You kind of get used to it, in a way. I mean, you did. So did Victor. But when you see things like child trafficking, an entire population destroyed by drugs and the crimes that come out of that are... Well, they're not average. What people will do to survive has always been a surprise to me, and trust me, it's dark."

"You should talk about it."

"Maybe I should... I could talk about anything to you, Cory. I promise, one day I will tell you about it, ok? But for now, I think we need to focus, or we'll have no vacation whatsoever."

He took my hand and led me towards the large tent. I could still see the cooking stations as we approached the entrance. They were empty and stark. The table where the judges sat still remained at the front of the stage. Alex had died only a few feet from us, and we had a front seat view.

"This place feels so different now. It was fun ..." Jensen's glance made me giggle as he rolled his eyes. "Ok, maybe boring, too. I never knew cooking shows would be so... basic."

"We watched people bake cakes. On TV it's thirty minutes. That was over two hours." Jensen walked up onto the stage and looked out at the empty audience seating. "We have to wait for the tox screen, but from what we saw, it had to be some kind of poison. The frothing of the mouth, his hands around his neck – not being able to breathe, those are textbook signs of poisoning. The question is how and when. Poisons can be fast, but the amount of poison would have to be quite large to work in less than an hour."

"We also have to ask ourselves if it was an accident, don't we?" I glanced around the empty tent. It made me shiver. I had the same kind of thing happen in empty theatres when I was alone. This space was designed to be full of people. Now it felt haunted and cold.

"An accident would have been Lily Tomlin putting rat poison in the coffee. The kind of poison they used was a deliberate act. Whatever it was, it was strong and meant to be deadly. Poisons don't usually act that fast. At least, not the kind of poisons you can find readily available. We'll know after they do the screening. I might need to call in a few favors to see if we can get that rushed."

"When we get back home, can we watch 9 to 5? That movie is fantabulous!" I needed something to look forward to. I was bummed about losing my time off to another investigation. It did seem to follow us around, but death was around everyone all the time. It was us who couldn't walk away from it. Maybe it was the rush of solving a mystery that had crept into our skin like a cancer, or maybe we were just way too nosy for our own good. I was definitely nosy.

"I promise. We just have to make sure that the FBI can get those samples and give them back to us fast. In a place like this... It could take months, and we don't have that kind of time." Jensen pouted, and my heart exploded with all of the emotions I had for him. He was so big and strong that when he did something like this, I found it adorable.

"Do you know who you can call?"

"I have a buddy in the Denver office. That would be the fastest – but that's a big if."

"What are y'all talking about?" Sheriff Roy shuffled in and stood at the edge of the entrance. "MacLeery is getting one of the production heads down here. Woke his ass up. Should be here in about thirty."

"Good. Thank you. We were talking about the tox screen."

"Oh, I have that covered. It's already in Denver. An old friend of my dad's is running the office. I may not be used to dealing with this kind of thing, but I know everyone in the area. If you boys had said no, I would have asked them for assistance. The coroner is running a few tests too, but Denver will give us more conclusive information."

"You mean we had an out, and you didn't tell us?" I huffed.

"Well... Making the call and getting them to take the case are two different things. I also hate to get the Feds involved in small-town business. They run rampant over everything." He took his hat off and held it tightly. By this time, I wasn't even sure why he wore the damn thing. Roy was not a fashionista, that's for sure. I would have cocked that brim and made it stylish.

Jensen looked over at me, and his eyes narrowed. Jensen? Let's take a quick walk through the back and see if anything stands out to us." It was better to pull him away from whatever was angering him than let him unleash on the sheriff. He nodded and glanced back at the sheriff. "We'll be back, Roy."

I walked up onto the stage and put my arm through his. He grasped my hand.

"Loosen your jaw, handsome. What's done is done." I whispered.

"We gave up our time, and he..."

"*We* gave up our time, is all you need to say. The choice was ours."

"We didn't quite have all of the information, though, did we? He's right about the Feds..."

"I'm not exactly happy about it, either – but we need to put that away and focus on the –"

"How am I the luckiest man in the world?"

I giggled and leaned into him as we crossed through the curtain and into the back area. "You knew a good thing when you saw one. I did too."

He turned and took me in his muscular arms and bent his head down. My leg popped before his lips ever touched mine. Soulful... the kiss rocked me to my very core, as it always did. His strong arms – my hands wrapped around his massive shoulders – his breath hot and sweet... Yeah, I was so in love; it was all-encompassing.

When he slowly broke away from me, he chuckled and shook his head. "You have no idea what you do to me."

I held up my engagement ring. "We have years for me to find out."

"Alright... Where are we? Wasn't this where we met the director and producer?"

"Yes, and where we saw how frosty they could be to our dead chef. Alex didn't seem to be very well-liked."

"He's known for being a total dick."

"Then you should have loved him," Jensen smirked, and I punched him on the arm.

"You'll pay for that." I winked.

"I'm hoping."

"I wonder how much time he spent back here? It couldn't have been much, not after the show started, anyway. They were keeping the judges in seclusion so they couldn't see who was baking what, remember?"

"No. That entire thing is a blur. I daydreamed about something a lot more exciting."

"Yeah... Figures."

"You were there... In my daydream."

"Were we on a beach?"

"You were saying, 'I do,' and I was staring into your beautiful eyes."

I blushed and walked over to him. "I will."

He took me in his arms again, and our lips slowly touched.

"He's here." Roy burst through the curtain. Now I was the one who wanted to commit murder.

"Oh, seems like I interrupted something."

I held up my ring. "Newly engaged." As if that explained why we were making out in the back of the tent. If he hadn't burst through... Kidding. I'm not that easy.

"Well, anyways... Congratulations." Roy said happily as he stood there. Jensen and I slowly broke away from each other, the electric current that held us slowly breaking.

"Thank you." Jensen stared at the man with the annoyance I felt. That bumbling Hallmark sheriff just prevented me from a kiss. That I would hold against him.

"Macleery," Sheriff Roy stepped aside. "Meet Jensen and Cory, the consultants I told you about."

"Good morning," Jensen and I said as one and then looked at each other and smiled.

"Morning, boys. I got Randy here out of bed." Macleery was a tall and very thin man with wild, curly, red hair hanging down into his face. Another man walked through the curtain with a cup of coffee he had to get from the hotel. He looked sleepy, and his short hair stuck up in the back from sleeping on it. I guess when they say they woke him up, they meant it.

"Hi. The deputy here said you needed a tour guide?" Randy looked as tired as I felt. He had dark circles under his eyes.

"It would help. Sheriff, do you have a list of everything that was bagged and boxed with you?"

"I got it here, along with the notes from the investigation." MacLeery walked over, and Jensen took the notes and nodded his thanks. "Not too much there, except for the contents. There was a lot of crap around here. Took us all evening and late into the night to bag it all."

Jensen looked at the list and frowned. "That's... Well, a lot. I assumed it would be." He sighed heavily. "Thanks for coming down and meeting us. We need to understand what all of these small sections backstage were for and what might have been in them. See if we can find something there that shouldn't have been, perhaps."

"Where would you like to start? Behind us are the holding quarters for the judges and their small makeup and dressing rooms. This is the backstage area where most of the crew stayed during the show, along with the director, as he called shots. To the other side is the same kind of set-up for the contestants." Randy pointed as he explained in his very rumpled clothes. He must have grabbed them from the floor and put them back on.

"Let's start where Alex would have been. Did the judges have a separate entrance to the tent?" Jensen glanced around.

"No. Everyone had a different entry time to keep the judges and contestants separate. Bakers came thirty minutes before the judges, and they were taken right to their own seclusion so they couldn't see each other."

"We know that Alex broke out of his quarters, at least once, anyway. We saw it with our own eyes."

"He left the judges section a few times to come and scream at Mike or Ry. He seemed to get off on it." Randy shrugged. "We're all used to dealing with it, even if it is annoying."

"So, most of you had worked with Alex before?" I interjected quickly.

"Not the locals who we were using, of course. The rest of us have been working off and on with the production company for years, so yeah, we all knew him. Knew all of them, actually. Bobbi is a favorite of everyone. But Alex started out as a diva and has only gotten worse. I spent one year on his show and transferred as fast as I could. May he rest in peace. He makes... well, made everyone's life hell."

"It's right through that curtain. We didn't install fake walls or anything for a one-day event. We just hung fireproof black drapes to keep everyone where they belonged." Randy walked us over to the entryway, which we had departed only a day before, and we followed behind, entering through the curtains into the holding room where we had met all of the judges.

"What was this main room for?" Jensen looked at the list.

"Just holding – the furniture is still here."

"Cheese plate, fruit, and a few beverages. Looks like water bottles and cans. All bought for the event, correct?"

"Yes. We used the Chalet's catering for the event." Randy leaned against the table that stood in the middle of the room. "We usually use trailers for this kind of thing, but we decided it wasn't worth it and did this instead."

"What else is there to see back here?" I walked around the space. It was just a place they sat and talked. We had seen it for ourselves.

"Dressing rooms are behind that large curtain. A four-by-four space for them to change clothes and have their makeup done." Randy walked over and pulled a curtain. "This was Alex's."

Jensen and I walked over and looked at the space. He glanced at the list and frowned. "Lots of makeup. I assume that their show clothes were hung up in here on the small rack, or did Alex wear his outfit when he arrived?"

"I wouldn't know. You'd have to ask one of the other judges or the makeup girl. We're all staying at the Pleasant Inn, except for the judges who are at the chalet with the producer and director." Randy glanced around the room and shivered. "It's just weird, you know. Alex was a class A dick, but... Who hated him enough to want him dead. I mean, we all saw the way he... It was horrible."

"That's what we're here to find out." I sounded sadder than I felt. I didn't know him, but to watch a man die in front of you, even if you didn't know that's what was happening at first, was... It was hard. For those that knew him, it was painful.

"Do they really use all this makeup?" Jensen perused the list and flipped the page. "It looks like each judge and contestant had their own makeup bin that's filled with all kinds of things."

"Yeah, production buys the kits, but not everything is used. If the seal was broken, that means it was probably used. Some makeup people break the seal on everything so they can keep it. Our production company has a strict rule of not sharing between cast members."

"That looks like everything that... It's all makeup and food in this room." Jensen glanced at me. I knew what he was pondering.

"It's possible. Vicki wrote about poisoned blush once, and there have been cases in real life. But if what was truly used was new and unopened... We'd have to make sure."

"The toxicology included skin samples, I hope? Do you know if those were taken from the face?"

"It's there in the notes towards the back. The coroner left a detailed memo of what was sent."

Jensen flipped back and read it quickly. "Good. That will help to rule out anything back here."

"Where did you store the leftover food?"

"There was no cheese or crackers left, only a little fruit, and it's labeled and stored at the station for now," Sheriff Roy said happily, as if this deserved a gold star.

"Sheriff, how good is your contact at the FBI? Could they send a lab tech here? That would expedite everything. We're going to need to test anything that was used or eaten by him from this area, as well as..." He glanced down. "Shit... Look at all of those ingredients."

"Did the contestants submit recipes?"

"I... not sure, actually. Some shows like this do have the recipes on file, and some don't. Depends on the show. You would have to ask Michael about that."

"Michael? The producer..." Jensen nodded. "Alright. I think that gives us a lot to work with. Or nothing at all.

Sheriff? Can you please make that call and get a tech here as soon as possible?"

"I'll make the call now." He nodded and walked out to the backstage area.

Randy took us over to the other side of the tent where the contestants were kept. The setup was smaller but a lot of the same. Dressing rooms and a small holding area. The main difference was here, there had never been food, only bottled water. It felt just as sterile and unexceptional.

"Randy? You said you worked with Alex? Could you tell us or put a checkmark by anyone else who had worked with him in the past?" I said as we made our way back to the stage.

"Sure could. There's a few of us here that's worked with him in the past on a show or two."

Jensen gave him a pen, and he looked over the list of staff and put a red check mark by the names of the people who had once worked with the fiery celebrity chef.

"We will need every surface that Alex may have been near tested as soon as the tech gets here." Jensen turned to the sheriff as he fumbled his way toward us.

"Good news. The deputy director, who was a friend of my dad's, will send one to help with the investigation later today. If you give me a list, I'll make sure that MacLeery shares it with him."

"Give me a second." Jensen jotted down the list for the sheriff and handed it to him. "I think the next thing we have to do is talk to these people? Can we have them come down to the station?"

"Consider it done. I'll have Gates give everyone a call and see if we can't get the first person to come in an hour."

"Great, schedule everyone in thirty-minute interviews. That will give us a chance to get through everyone, for now."

Jensen glanced over at me and smiled. "Until then, we can have an hour to wander around town."

"That sounds very good." I knew he was trying to give me a moment of normalcy on our vacation. It made me feel warm and cozy to know how much he cared about me. I had prayed for a long time to find a man like Tom Jensen, and here he was standing with me, loving me with everything he had.

"It's not that big a town, but here's the address to the station. It's only two blocks over from the park." Roy pointed. "It overlooks the lake and has a very pretty view."

Jensen nodded and took my hand. It was the best hour of my day so far.

5

The Sheriff's station looked nothing like the one in Maple Bay, which was much more modern and organized. Point Pleasant's was small and had four rooms. One of those rooms held the only jail cell in town. It was quaint and cute as if a shabby chic designer had brought in every piece of furniture and décor.

The room where we waited to interview the people who knew Alex was small but decorated like a small sitting room. A couch sat along one wall with a couple of chairs around a coffee table. This was way too cozy for an interrogation room. This was a place you curled up and looked out at the blue lake and read a book with a cup of tea.

"This town is unreal." Jensen chuckled deeply. "Seriously, like… This room is… Harper would lose his mind."

"Victor would get the heebie-jeebies from the décor alone. That fake tree would drive him to a small breakdown. Not doing too much for me either. They haven't had anyone dust in here in the last decade."

"This is more of a breakroom than anything else. Could you live in a place like this? Everything seems so…"

"I told you. It's a town that only lives on television. And yes, I think I could."

"Me too. One day maybe."

"Seems like a perfect place to retire or something like it. I'd miss the ocean, though."

"Yeah. I couldn't' surf very easily here. But I think I could relax. Maybe find a place like this and become its chief or sheriff one day."

"One day... Maybe." We looked deeply into each other's eyes. The future of us hanging between us.

A knock on the door caught us both off guard.

"Boys, I have Sarah Walton waiting outside. Are you ready?" Gates was an exceedingly handsome black man with a torso that threatened to pop open his tight shirt with every move. His shaved head and tight beard only made him more handsome.

Jensen looked down at the notes. "Makeup... Thanks' Gates. Please have her come in."

A short, middle-aged woman with light grey hair walked into the room in a large pink muumuu that flowed behind her. Even with a full beat on her face, she looked tired. Makeup couldn't hide the grief that showed in her red-rimmed eyes.

"Thank you for meeting us so quickly, Sarah. Please have a seat," Jensen said compassionately. He, too, was a good judge of people, and I trusted his instincts. Mine told me, right away, that this woman was no killer. The lip liner alone was on point.

Sarah sat down on the cushy couch and nestled into it. She kicked off her shoes and pulled her legs up underneath her. She wasted no time getting comfortable.

"I understand. I'm just in shock that this... happened." She looked down at her clenched hands and bit her bottom lip as if she were battling back her emotions. "Sorry... It's been a very hard couple of days."

"You work for the production company?" Jensen asked and leaned forward in his chair.

She shook her head. "No. I work... worked exclusively with Alex. I've been his makeup and hair technician for nine years. When he got his first show on television, I met him that first day, and I've never left his side. Where Alex goes, if he's being filmed, I go too. Went... I guess. I went too."

"Did you do the makeup of the other guests on his show?"

"No. There are... There was a makeup team who handled everyone else. The only person I do makeup for is... was Alex."

I stood up and walked over to the door, and opened it. "One second, please." I glanced down at her. "Gates? Do you have a box of tissue?"

Gates nodded and got out of his seat to hand me a box of generic brand tissue from his desk. I bet it felt like sandpaper. I nodded my thanks and shut the door before placing the tissue box on the arm of the couch.

"Thank you..." She managed as she reached out to take one.

"You and Alex must have been close." I could see it in the way she talked about him. She had cared for him in some way.

"Alex was... difficult? Everyone thought so – but he and I had something that the rest of them didn't have. He trusted me to do my job and to make him look better than he actually did. I trusted him too. After a few years of working together, we both felt a loyalty to each other. I mean, he paid my son's way through UCLA. When he cared about you, he could be very generous." She blew her nose and then balled the tissue up in her hand.

"Did you and Alex talk a lot? Did he confide in you about things, or was your... relationship not that... type?" Jensen struggled to get out what was in his head.

"I think he told me everything. I was there when he thought he was falling in love and then invariably when it was over. He told me about any show drama that was happening or if something was off in his life. Actors, celebrities... I guess it's the same for everyone... When you sit down in a beautician's chair or a barber's... You talk. Most times, you say more than you ever mean to. It's a part of the job of a hairstylist or makeup artist to listen to the client. With Alex, we shared quite a bit with each other over the years." She reached up and wiped a tear from her eyes. "My family was invited to his house for parties, dinners – We spent Thanksgiving there."

"Did he recently mention anything that made him feel unsafe?"

"He always felt unsafe. Alex was fueled by anxiety and anger. Always has been. That's one of the things that made him a great chef, I think. That inability to be mediocre, and he demanded the same commitment from anyone he worked with." She paused and laughed sadly. "A lot of reality shows are scripted. Did you know that? But not with Alex. His show was raw and what was actually happening in his kitchens. Alex was the catalyst – his own way of being that made the magic of his show so watchable. If you were in his kitchen, you would do something wrong that raised his ire. It was inevitable. No one could live up to the standards he expected – that he demanded of himself, except for Alex. It was magical."

"But besides that... Anyone who maybe had threatened him or gotten into an argument?"

"Everyone he has ever met has gotten into an argument with him. But the kind of argument that would lead to murder... No, not that I know of." She answered thoughtfully – sadly, even. She understood her boss and seemed to also understand his weaknesses.

"From what you know... Is there anyone on this production that might have had a beef with Alex that remained... unresolved? An old argument that might have led to a deeper hurt?"

"That's... Maybe. I mean, Michael worked for a few years on Alex's show. They used to get into screaming matches on set. But Michael has worked with quite a few temperamental celebrities over the years. I'm sure he was used to it. A couple of the crew members had been on and off the show for years. Same thing. I've seen Alex make an electrician cry as he berated him for using a colored gel he didn't like. Sorry... I don't think I know of anything that is truly helpful."

"One last question. The makeup that you used... I mean, you've been his makeup artist for years. Did you use any of your own makeup, or was it all from the production?"

"Production. When they offer to buy you whatever makeup you want, and you get to keep it afterward, only a fool would insist on bringing their case. Even the brushes I used were out of the package."

"Alright, I think that's all we have, Sarah? As a reminder, I have to let you know that anyone involved with the production will be told when they can leave town."

"Do you know when that might be?"

"In this state, they can only hold for seventy-two hours

once you've been notified. After that, if you are not a person of interest, they can't keep you here any longer."

"Oh, one last question, please, if you don't mind. Did Alex change clothes after arriving, or did he wear his outfit to the venue?" I asked, remembering quickly that it was something that we might need to know. Who the hell knew at this point?

"I don't know. He got there before me, but... I don't remember seeing any other clothes in his dressing room, so I would think he wore them there. I can't be sure, though." She shrugged.

I stood up. "Sarah... I just want to say that I'm sorry for your loss. If Alex paid for your son's college tuition, he cared a lot for you."

"Yes. I did him, too. Find the killer and give me five minutes alone with him. I want to make whoever did this pay. He might have been an asshole, and lord knows he was. But he was my friend."

6

The day continued with interviewing the rest of the crew. The comments from most of them were the same. They were grips, lighting, sound, and food assistants that had worked with him on at least one project. A few of them had been on Alex's show for one season or more. It seemed to be an incestuous group that traveled from show to show with the same production company.

One of the things I hadn't known was that the production company that had most of the shows on the network paid for everything themselves and got a check from the network when the shows were delivered. I had always assumed that the network itself paid for the cost of production. It seemed a weird way to do business. What if they decided to not buy the show after it was delivered? What if they didn't like the final project? I had a lot of questions, and none of them were about the murder.

I needed to do a twirl, change my shoes and get my head on straight. I had imagined this weekend as a time to let my proverbial hair down and let loose with some friends. Now I was embroiled in a television scandal. A celebrity chef murdered while filming a reality competition show was going to be big news.

I kept searching for it online, and by the middle of the day, the story had broken on every media outlet. TMZ was having a field day with his untimely demise. If you googled his name now, the only thing you would find is that he had died, and the cause of death was under investigation. I'm sure TMZ would love the fact that Jensen and I were the ones doing the investigation, and we weren't even from here.

We didn't have much time before the media descended and turned this entire town into a circuit party as they interviewed anyone and everyone who saw what happened. We had to finish our investigation fast, or the truth would get muddied by the press quicker than a press-on nail usually popped off.

"How far is it to the Chalet?" I asked Gates as he drove us up the winding mountain road in his jeep.

"Another five minutes or so." He glanced at us in the rearview mirror.

I sat snuggled up against Jensen with his arm around me. His fingers stroked my arm. It had become our thing whenever we cuddled on the couch. His fingertips lightly brushed against my skin, making me mad with desire. Soon... Very soon, we would be tied forever.

The moment he met me, he fell head over heels in love. That's what he tells me, and I guess it's true. It took me a bit. I mean, when I first saw him, I almost fell down a set of stairs. This tall bo-hunk standing there looking better than a man should in his deputy costume. That face was so chiseled and handsome that it might have made my head spin. Not to mention the muscles that covered every inch of his tight and overly sexy body. We had to sit together in a stakeout, and with every word we spoke to each other, we let our defenses down. By the end of that heinous and incredibly gross case – we both knew that there was something between us.

That grew quickly.

Even the thought of a life without Jensen made me want to walk away from being the fabulous diva I was. I don't think I could survive if something happened to him. I'm not as strong as Victor, no matter how hard I try. I'm not as sure of my place in the world as Harper, even though I feel more secure than ever. But Tom Jensen made me believe in a happy ever after. He showed me how it could be true with every glance, touch, and smile that he beamed down upon me.

Love wasn't just a sappy thing that pop divas sang about. It was real, and I was in the throes of a very amazing case of it. I think… I hoped it was completely incurable.

"What did we learn so far today?" Jensen sighed heavily. "He wasn't very well-liked. We knew that already. He was a bit of a prima donna."

"We knew that too. We also learned that he could be kind when he wanted. What he did for his makeup girl Sarah was wonderful. She used all new makeup, according to her. We'll have to have the field officer verify whatever he can about that, just to be sure. Anything opened has to be tested for toxins."

"I think everything has to be tested. The size of that list… The ingredients that were in the kitchen for them to use was huge. One technician could spend days testing everything, and we don't have that kind of time." He cracked his neck. He did that sometimes when he was tense. He had a very sexy neck.

"We have to narrow the list down then. Makeup, the food in the holding room, and any ingredient that was used during the competition that he would have ingested? Are we missing anything? I think that if we can find out where the poison was, it would narrow the list of who had access to it down, wouldn't it?"

"You know a lot more about Hollywood than I do." Jensen chuckled. "We can ask Blake. Maybe he can help us."

"We will have to interview him. He had his own space, he said. Funny that we weren't shown that, though. We'll have to ask him." Why didn't Randy even mention Blake's dressing room? I mean, we forgot about him too. But he was on stage, and even if he was our friend, we would have to treat him the same way we were looking at everyone else.

"Blake never got too close to the stations. He kept his distance most of the time. Whenever he was near them, he talked and mugged to the audience. All eyes were on him, so I think we can easily rule him out. He wasn't with the other judges before the show. It really comes down to timing with a poisonous substance."

"What do you mean?"

"Remember the poisoned water during the drag pageant. It wasn't instantaneous. The poison took time to elicit a reaction. Alex didn't seem to feel bad during the judging. It hit him quickly. That means it had to be a very large and lethal dose to affect him in a matter of seconds... Or he was poisoned earlier, and it had to take time to work through his system. I think that's the key, and no matter what we do, we have to wait for the forensic autopsy and the technician to find any trace of a foreign substance."

"Does that mean we can meet Danny and Blake for a drink tonight?"

"I think we're going to need it."

"Look at that." I pointed ahead of us. Jensen took his eyes off me, and I felt instantly bereft. I had it bad.

The Point Pleasant Chalet stood before us in all of its grand glory. It was a large and ornate building that shown brightly from the valley it set it. The glass windows sparkled in the sun, and the snow that surrounded it seemed completely out of place since it was summer.

"How is there snow?" I was baffled.

"It's man-made. They keep the front of the chalet looking freshly snowed in every morning. They spray the powder all over the bottom of the ski range. Snows still real for most of the year towards the top." Gates laughed, and his dark eyes sparkled.

"Do you want me to come with you, or do you think having me in there will be problematic?"

"We got this," I answered quickly.

"Actually, I think it might be best for Gates to be with us. These people are high-powered, and having someone with an actual badge from this town might be helpful. Might keep them on their toes and throw them off." Jensen shrugged as Gate's pulled the car up to the front.

"My favorite part of having a badge is never looking for a parking spot."

"I call that Doris Day parking." I giggled.

"Why is it called that?" Jensen unbuckled his seat belt.

"I have absolutely no idea. Maybe they reserved her a parking space or something wherever she went? I've just always heard it. Victor says it every now and then." I took my seatbelt off too, and started to open my door.

"What would you call it if you had never heard that before? What's a very Cory way of saying the same thing?" Jensen touched me on the leg, and I felt the heat of his palm through my pink linen pants.

"I don't know... Sissy spaces? A spot reserved just for me."

"I think I'd call it Cory's car spot." He smiled.

"We'll have to work on your sass." I frowned.

"I think you like me as I am. If I were as sassy as you, where would we be?" He winked and turned to get out of the car. I put my hand on his shoulder and stopped him.

"I prefer you butch. That lets me be the catty one. It's my best quality besides my ass."

"I love you, babe."

"Ditto, and I love when you call me babe. Never stop that. Let's go."

We got out of the car and walked hand in hand to the Chalet.

7

"Where are they?" Gal's larger-than-life presence came into the room before she did. "Oh, over here, I think."

"Ladies." Gate's deep voice greeted them as he stood near the door. Gal and Bobbi entered together and smiled as they walked over to us.

The Sheriff had set up a small conference room for us to speak to everyone staying at the Chalet. It was ok to ask the crew to come down to the station, but he didn't want to cause a PR nightmare with the celebrities since the news had broken on the internet. We sat at one side of a large wooden table, and Gal and Bobbi took the seats on the other side.

"What are you two doing here? Aren't you friends with Blake?" Gal grinned widely as she shifted in her seat.

"Don't you remember what Blake told us? I swear you'd forget your own name if your ego wasn't so big." Bobbi cackled. "The muscly one is a cop, and the cute one in the fabulous outfit is Vickie Dean's assistant. They're the ones who solved that mystery at the…"

"You solved the murder of Marcus Montrose! I remember the headlines. Yes, Blake told us about that horrifying weekend when we all had dinner the night before." Gal slapped the table. "I hadn't forgotten. I was just tipsy."

"How many of you had dinner that night?" Jensen asked jovially, trying to keep them talking.

"Oh, it was just the judges and Blake. Everyone else was busy getting everything ready. It was my idea. None of us had ever met Blake before, and he's an actual star. It's not often we get someone of his caliber hosting one of these gigs. He's very sweet." Gal answered. "He's also devastatingly handsome."

"So are these two." Bobbi winked at us. "Why are all the hot guys gay? The story of my life."

"You? I married one." Gal shrugged. "Still the best husband I've ever had, and I've had four."

"I know you boys didn't ask to meet with us to talk about our failed relationships. You're here to ask us about Alex. Shoot. I'll tell you anything I know." Bobbi said solemnly, bringing the festivities of gossip to an end. I could have sat here and listened to them all night.

I cleared my throat and glanced at Jensen. He knew I was still star-struck around Gal. I was a celebrity whore.

"We're interviewing anyone who had worked with him before or was in the vicinity of him during the competition," Jensen said politely. "We're trying to get a timeline of everything so we can piece together what we know. You two seem very chummy, and it appeared you were with Alex, too. Did you arrive all together?"

"Well, I wouldn't say that we were chummy with Alex." Gal dropped her voice. "I've been a judge on his show a few times, and he's made a few appearances on mine. The same could be said for Bobbi here. The difference between Bobbi and Alex is Bobbi is an actual friend of mine. Alex was someone I worked with every now and then. We would see each other at events thrown by the network every now and then, but chummy? No. Very few people would ever say they were chummy with Alex."

"I knew him better than most of the others, I guess. Out of all the... personalities on the network, I'm probably the most uncomfortable with public appearances. I think Alex liked that I didn't take all of this too seriously. I've never had a restaurant like most of them. I was just a home cook who got lucky."

"A very great home cook," I said quickly and felt like an idiot. "You taught me how to dice an onion and make chicken noodle soup."

"I'm glad, sweetheart. A hot ass can get you a boyfriend, but a meatloaf will help you keep him." She winked and smiled happily at me. "Alex always had this... competition, I guess, with Gal and most of the others. They all own restaurants and came from a culinary school where they studied and of that bullshit." Bobbi glanced over at Gal, who smirked back at her. "Gal understands. Alex took it all very seriously. If he opened a new restaurant, it was always in Los Angeles or New York City, and it always had to get better reviews than whoever on the network opened the last eatery. He wanted to win, even if there wasn't really a competition to win."

"That sums it up a whole lot nicer than anyone else would have ever said." Gal nodded. "It's why Bobbi's my actual friend and not just someone I know. That's how most people viewed Alex. Someone they occasionally worked with and had to be friendly to twice a year when the network threw a bash. Most people thought he was a pompous ass."

"Well, he was a pompous ass. Bless his heart. He thought his shit didn't stink, and we all know that's not how life works."

"What was the question?" Gal shrugged. "Oh! Did we all come together? Yes, the car came and picked us all up at once."

"Did you all wear your show clothes there, or did you change at the venue?" I said way too seriously, and Gal grinned.

"I think we all wore our clothes down, hon. I did, and I don't remember Alex changing."

"He didn't." Bobbi shook her head as she looked over at her friend. "Remember? I commented on the fact that he wasn't wearing a tie." She glanced over at us. "He usually wore one, but he said since it was a stupid concept, he didn't want to appear that he cared too much. They offered us an outrageous amount of money to come to judge this special event. It was supposed to be the kickoff of their small-town weekend on the channel. This show will now never see the light of day. Hell, we didn't even choose a winner."

"Who would you have chosen?"

"I don't know. I never even took a bite of the last cake."

"That's funny. Neither did I?"

"What was the last cake? I don't remember?" Jensen said almost to himself.

"It was the Pandam cake. It looked beautiful and had such a nice aroma. I was pushing in on the cake with my fork noticing the spongy texture, which was perfect when Alex started having his fit." Bobbi's voice dropped to a whisper. "Poor thing. I can't believe he's gone." She sniffed back her emotions.

"Me either. I didn't exactly like the mother fucker, but I didn't dislike him either. He was just Alex. You took him as he was. His shows were very successful, and I hate that all of those people are going to be out of a job. It's horrible." Gal reached over at patted Bobbi's knee. "You have such a huge heart Bobbi Day."

"I have a huge ass." She elbowed Gal.

"Me too, girl. Me too."

"Did you both eat from the cheese and fruit tray?" Jensen continued.

"We ate the whole thing, almost. Alex didn't touch it. We kept teasing him about helping us out." Bobbi slumped. "I told him he was too skinny and should help a couple fat ladies out."

"He was drinking from his flask, though." Gal looked over her shoulder after saying it. "I caught him a couple times when he didn't think we were looking. Not sure what it was, really. I'm assuming vodka because his breath didn't really have a spirit smell if you know what I mean."

"I didn't notice that. I was cramming my face full of cheese and crackers." Bobbi shrugged. "When this is over, do you want to go down and grab something? I'm feeling a bit peckish, and I don't think we'll be able to go down into town since the story leaked. I'm sure those vultures are about to swarm."

"Yeah. We're going to be stuck in here until we can leave. I don't feel like being a sound bite about the death of one of our own."

"Did Alex ever say anything to you that may allude that he was worried? Anything about someone that may be out to get him in some way?" I asked and leaned forward, waiting for them to say the magic words that would let me finish my vacation in peace.

"Honey, Alex didn't confide in us about anything. If he had someone that... he liked that much, I don't know them."

Gal looked at me sadly. "Would someone want to kill Alex? Of course. Would they? That's a very different bird of a feather, isn't it? Do you know how many chefs, kitchen workers, waitstaff, food runners, producers, and directors he had fired over his career? The list is endless."

"You should talk to Michael. He worked with him the most out of anyone, I guess. He was his producer for quite some time." Bobbi nodded as if that settled everything. "He and Alex had a tumultuous relationship, but I guess they were still in good... that they were still friendly. I know that Alex was the first judge Michael brought on."

"Is that everything? Cory, honey, I'm happy to give you my number if you think of anything else. And if you're ever in LA, let me know, and I'll have you both as my guest at Gal's On The Square."

She gave me her number and then she stood up.

"Time to eat?" Bobbi raised her hand, and Gal pulled her up out of the chair. "Good luck. I think you boys are going to need it."

8

We only waited a few minutes before a knock happened on the open door. "Am I early?" Ry stood there looking thinner than a hungry model. His deep-set eyes and unruly blonde hair were even more of a train-wreck than they were last night. "I just want to get this over with."

"Actually, we have Michael Vickers coming in next. Just waiting for him to arrive." Gates crossed his arms, and his stare made the thin man seem to shrink even more.

"Normally, I wouldn't interview people together, but... Maybe if they get talking, we'll learn something more than we expected." Jensen whispered. "The ladies were very chatty together."

"You know these are my first interrogations, right?" I snorted.

I wouldn't give myself an A for what I've added. But I think Victor would be proud of what I've done so far. He may not be in the force like Harper and Jensen, but Victor had one of the quickest minds I had ever met. As mystery writer Vicki Dean, he had a brain that was meant to solve puzzles, and that's exactly what murder was whenever you tried to put it together piece by piece. He wasn't only my best friend, but I kind of idolized him. I had placed him on a pedestal long before I ever knew his secret.

"Come on in and have a seat. As long as it's fine with Mr. Vickers, we're ok with it, too." Jensen offered and pointed to the seat in front of us. "Are you doing ok?"

"Sure. This was supposed to be the biggest break I ever had, and now no one will ever see it. Who's going to want to hire the man who directed the death of Alex Topacheffi?" He looked at us with wide eyes. He was panicking. This was not the panic of a murderer. It was someone watching their life implode around them.

"Oh, I think you'd be surprised. You may even get an Emmy." Michael Vickers stood in the doorway with his hand on the sill. His thin mustache was just as annoying to me as ever. Really, if he was a lady, she would have waxed that shit off her upper lip. Michael walked in calmly and sat down in the chair beside Ry. "It's not that bad. No one's going to blame you or hold it against you. I'd hire you again, and I'll make sure that everyone at the network knows."

"I never really watch the credits at the end of these types of shows." I realized as the words tumbled from my pouty lips.

"No one ever does. That's why the credits shrink to a tiny, little, minuscule size so the network can use that time for free promo of another show." Michael laughed.

"Is there one director for each show that sees production through the season? Or is it more like primetime scripted where there are many directors for each series?" Now I was actually curious. I wasn't sure how it was helping us solve the case, but I was getting a lesson in Hollywood. Hey, at least it would keep them talking.

"No. If we had the same director for an entire season of a cooking show, they would commit suicide by the end. It's honestly the same show over and over, isn't it? Do you watch a lot of these shows?" Michael nodded, already knowing the answer. "Are they not the same?"

How had I never noticed that? Was I that vapid? "Yeah... I guess they are. Gal's Games has different challenges on every show, but..."

"The format remains the same forever. Exactly. Gal has two challenges on every show. There are three contestants, and one contestant gets cut after the first challenge. Almost all of these shows have the exact same format. Even the judges hop around from one show to another. The contestants do too. One day they are on Top Chef, then a month later, they're on a different one. Alex's show was the same every year too. A diva chef screaming and yelling and firing people who want the opportunity to work in his kitchen. Do you know how many of those winners still worked for Alex? One. One after nine seasons of his theatrics and throwing things. A director would lose his mind if he had to do an entire season of one of those shows." Michael grinned. He didn't seem to be nearly as jittery today as he did at the taping.

"Isn't that just life, though?" Jensen looked puzzled. "We all go through the same format of our daily lives. For most people, it's wake up, work, eat dinner, and go to bed, to get up and do the same thing all over again."

"Mundanity? Yes, I agree. For most people, their life revolves around their home, commute time, work, commute time, and then a quick evening before they go to bed. But for an artist, that same existence that most normal people strive for is death. It prevents you from dreaming and looking for something new when you are mired in the normal."

"I was just glad to get this job. I've been making short films and then worked a couple seasons as an assistant director for a reality show about dating, which shall not be named. This was my shot at finally getting on the directing circuit for the company. I'm hoping that they…"

"I told you, Ry. You have nothing to worry about." Michael put his hand on Ry's shoulder and patted him hard.

"I'm assuming that since you're new, you've never worked with Alex or any of the others before?" I tried to pull us back to the tea that needed to be spilled.

"Never. This was my first production for the company. I got the job through having a few director friends who recommended me. This was like an audition. I got very lucky."

"You also had a very good reel. We chose you because we believed you could do it, and it's time for us to bring in some new blood. The slate of shows keeps expanding, and there is never enough staff to keep up with the production schedule. You'll be on a new show in no time. Trust me." Michael nodded vigorously - which made Ry relax a little. His shoulders which he had been using for ear muffs, lowered enough to realize he had a neck.

"You had worked with Alex, though, hadn't you?" Jensen looked up, and Michael paused, giving him his full attention.

"Of course. I've been with this company for quite some time. But I did work on Alex's show for a while. They brought me in when the ratings started to slump. I brought the show back from the brink of cancellation and made it a hit again by mixing things up a little."

"Altering the format?" Jensen asked and leaned back in his chair.

"A little. You can't alter it much because people know

what to expect, but a little surprise or shock every now and then makes them want to tune back in." He shrugged and crossed his legs.

"What was your relationship with Alex like?" I tried to make the question as mundane as possible. I failed. I might as well have stood up and pointed at him, screaming murderer.

Michael stiffened quickly. "Difficult - to say the least."

"You no longer work on his show. I remember you saying that you no longer worked for him when we first met you." Jensen was able to pull off the conversational tone a lot better than I did. Michael seemed to relax a little again. But his eyes darted as if he knew he was being considered as a suspect. I didn't have the heart to tell him that everyone was at this point? He wasn't special.

"Oh yes. I remember that. Alex was screaming about something. I learned to tune that out a long time ago. But I was the one who thought he would be a good fit for this show. People loved him, even if he was a giant prick." Michael uncrossed his legs and leaned forward with his elbows on his knees. "Alex could turn on a dime, but when it came to amateur cooks, he did a pretty great job making them feel like they accomplished something. He was quite good with those types of contestants and a total dictator when it came to the professionals."

"Was this show your idea?" I asked, actually curious.

"Oh, God, no." He laughed loudly. It reverberated through the bare room. "It was a great idea, though. One of the executives wanted to do this weekend of small-town cooking competitions with home chefs and bakers. This is just one of over a dozen shows that were supposed to be a part of that. The company was giving away over a million dollars in prize money all over the country. I was asked which show I wanted, and I chose one of the baking shows. Point Pleasant is a lot closer to LA than West Virginia or Michigan. This show was about logistics for me. I hate traveling."

"How did Gal and Bobbi come on board?" Jensen looked down at his notes. I glanced over and could barely read the chicken scratch he was writing. Seriously, Jensen had the handwriting of a blindfolded drug addict.

"Bobbi is doing all of the baking shows. She loves that genre and will be the one judge to tie them all together. She'll also be one of the faces they will use for publicity. Gal is scheduled for another somewhere on the East Coast with seafood home cooks or something like that." Michael grinned. "Bobbi was given to me, and I couldn't have been happier about that. She's a pro and a doll. Gal got to make her own choices as to which shows she would appear on. I'm the one who pitched Alex. I actually had to fight for him a little. The network was worried he would come across as too harsh."

Jensen set his pen down and slumped into his chair. "But you knew better…" He made it sound like praise. I was impressed by my hunky, almost hubby.

"After three seasons on his show… I lasted longer than any other producer he had ever had. I knew him enough to know he would be great, especially with Bobbi and Gal. They're both so sweet. I needed a little fire. Alex was as fiery as they got. But… Like I said, he was great with amateurs and wanted to make them feel like champions. I had seen it before. I knew he would be perfect, and the three of them together would have been the highest star power on any of the other judging panels. It was a win for everyone."

"Did Alex agree quickly?" I picked up Jensen's pen and

scooted his notes over to me. Someone had to write something that someone else could read.

Michael looked over at Ry and laughed. "Alex didn't agree quickly to anything. His agent negotiated a very nice package for him. He was even going to get a brand-new show. He would have had two primetime shows on the network because of his contract. He wanted guarantees, and he got them."

"Did you know that he would do that? That he would make negotiations on his own behalf?" I asked, trying to write notes as I looked at Michael. I glanced down and realized why Jensen's writing was so bad. Shit. I couldn't even read my own writing.

"They all make negotiations on their own behalf. It's business, and they pay their agents to be sharks. The more money a client makes, the more the agent makes. It's the game that's played in every contract negotiation. So, yeah. I expected it." He shrugged as if it were a normal thing.

"Uh... When did you leave Alex's show?" I used my sweetest voice, the pitch increasing to a dolphin's pitch.

Michael smiled at me. "Three months ago."

Jensen leaned forward. "When did these negotiations happen?"

"I was still on the show when all of this started. When the contracts were signed... I'm not sure. Pre-production is fast and furious. I didn't even know who my judges were until last month." He seemed so easy and smooth. But he seemed to know more about Alex than anyone else here.

"Why did you... uh... leave the show?" I glanced away from him. That felt way too pointed. Damn, this was a lot harder than I expected. Victor made it look so easy.

Michael took a moment and swallowed. "You'd have to ask Alex," he said sadly. "He fired me, as he had fired all of his previous producers before me. You've seen how he is in his kitchen. He likes the same kind of chaos within the production staff."

"So, Alex was the one with all the power when it came to his show?" It seemed important, but honestly, I was just intrigued. Why was I born a star fucker?

"It's that way for all of our star chefs. If they want something, they get it. Don't like the last director brought in? Then, they never come back. Same with the rest of the staff. Me included."

I glanced over at Jensen, who nodded at me to continue. This felt important for some reason. I just wished I understood why. "But you lasted longer than the others. Why was that?"

Michael snorted and crossed his arms as he bit his bottom lip in thought. Maybe he wasn't sure why, either? "The network was surprised when Alex didn't want to replace me at the end of my first year. Hell, I was too. I had heard how he was. But we had a good working relationship. I knew that he was what the show was all about, and I kept the focus on him. He liked that."

"You have no idea why he let you go?" Jensen asked more forcefully but still kept it light. He really was a master.

"No." Michael sounded like he was getting tired of answering our questions. "We never talked about it. I found out that I was moving to a different show after the season wrapped."

"Did you ever talk to Alex about it afterward?" I asked quickly, trying to keep him on his toes.

"No!" His shout made poor Ry almost fall out of his chair. He flinched so hard. "Like I said, we *never* talked about it. What would have been the point? I was ready to move on. I had been in the same show for three years and was tired of dealing with all the bullshit. I was given a new show right away. I didn't speak to Alex until I saw him yesterday. If I had known it would be the last time... I would have said more... I guess."

"What was Alex's new show?" This was gossip. I did gossip better than anyone. I leaned forward as if he were serving me the best dish ever. I mean, I'd never get to sample it, but it was still juicy details.

"Funnily enough. It's an amateur cooking competition with him as a mentor. He was going to go into people's homes and help them make a meal. Genius idea. Shame it will now never happen."

Jensen cleared his throat. "We need to ask a few questions about the show format that we saw yesterday. Who purchased the materials for the chefs, and how were they delivered?"

"Everything came from the warehouse where we store our food products. We use brand-new products for freshness, and the seals are all removed for easy access on the day of the taping. After this type of show, we find a charity to donate the used products to. They were brought in on one of the production trucks."

"So, every item used came from production?"

"Yep. Every single one."

"Who opened the food products?"

"Our food assistants. That's their only job is to choose and place the food items in the pantries."

"Did the contestants give you a shopping list?"

Michael looked at Jensen, perplexed.

"Recipes, he means," I interjected.

Michael grinned. "Oh, yeah. For this show, yes. They had to submit their recipes to be considered for the show. It was a part of the agreement that we had with the city's mayor for us to come film here. We could deny a contestant if their recipe didn't seem exciting enough. We turned away three bakers before we settled on the lady who baked the carrot cake. We asked them to send us a short video of them baking in their home, and hers was too funny to not cast her."

Ry chuckled. "She was so dry and sarcastic in her video. It was perfection. She really should have her own show where she drinks sherry and talks badly about her neighbors."

Jensen suppressed a laugh and placed his hands back on the table. I was furiously writing down all the notes, trying hard to keep up with the conversation. "We will need copies of those recipes, and if we can get their audition tapes, that might be helpful, too."

"I can send them right over? Should they go to the sheriff's station?"

"Yes, thank you. So, you made sure that the ingredients they requested were in place at their stations?"

"Exactly. This show was easy because we only had to bring what was on their recipe cards. Back in LA, when we stock a competition pantry, it has anything and everything that they might use. Those ingredients stay on the shelf through the run of the season except for fresh ingredients, which are replaced daily."

"Did the assistants keep a record of the ingredients? Like if a seal might have been broken?"

Michael stared at us before answering. I heard his tongue click on the roof of his mouth. "I don't... No. If something would have had its seal broken, they would have replaced it. We guarantee fresh ingredients. We have to. It's in the contract signed with the contestants. Our assistants in food and pantry are the best at what they do. They would never have done that."

Jensen sighed and glanced down at my notes. "Anything stand out as... weird to you?"

Michael sat back in his chair and grinned at us as if we were stupid. "It's show business. Everything is weird. What do you mean?"

"From the contestant's recipes or from their tapes?"

"Ok... No. They seemed like normal home bakers who wanted a chance at a hundred thousand. We didn't expect fireworks or drama since that wasn't what this show was about. It was about championing someone that reminded you of someone you know – your grandmother or father even. We were just surprised at how difficult the cakes were that two of the bakers wanted to make. Honestly, we were expecting one of them to fail. But she didn't. That's what this kind of show is about. Overcoming adversity and becoming a champion."

I slapped the table in my very own Oprah A-Ha moment. "What happens now that no one was declared a winner?"

Michael glanced over at Ry, who frowned.

"That is the million-dollar question, isn't it? Because the bakers held up their part of the bargain, there is a clause in the contracts put in for our insurance clause. All three of them will be awarded the prize money. The fault of a winner not being declared doesn't stand with the bakers. So, they all win – without winning."

Jensen's phone rang loudly, and he fished it out of his tight pants. He wore those just for me.

"One second," he said quickly while answering. "I think that's it, gentlemen. Thank you for your time, and we might contact you to ask some follow-up questions if we have any.

This was very enlightening. We appreciate the help you've given us."

Michael and Ry stood up, and Michael threw his arm around his glum friend. "I have time to grab a drink before I meet someone at the Inn. Wanna join me?" They walked out of the room.

"What is it, Sheriff? Yes, I mean Roy." Jensen rolled his eyes. "We will be there as soon as Gates can get us there." He hung up. "We have some results."

Gage drove down the mountain a lot faster than he drove up. By the time we got into town, my stomach was threatening to unload everything I hadn't eaten today.

Jensen grasped my hand all the way down. He knew that what we were about to find out would help us or make this impossible to solve.

We had no idea what we were about to be told. If we had, we would have had a drink first.

9

"You have to be shitting me?" Jensen sat down as if he were utterly exhausted, the pages of the coroners finding clutched tightly in his hand. "How can his body show signs of poisoning and no toxins were found? That's insane."

"Is it? Vicki wrote about a poisoning case that used an untraceable poison."

"That's fiction. Scientists can trace anything if they know what to look for. The cause of death is asphyxiation." Jensen glanced over at the coroner.

"Oh, God, not again," I said way too passionately. Our last vacation was destroyed by someone we thought was strangled to death.

"Hopefully, the FBI results on toxicology will reveal something that our equipment here couldn't detect. Poisons, all poisons leave a trace, but sometimes they are harder to find than others. Many poisons could lead to a coroner pronouncing death by asphyxiation. There are quite a few poisons that shut down the body in that exact way."

"We can rule out the cakes made by the first two contestants because all three judges ate them. Is there a poison that has to interact with something else to become deadly?"

"Of course. Some drugs can't be mixed, but that kind of poisoning would be slower and take time to build up in the body. Pharmacists have to be aware of every drug you take because some combinations can result in death."

"I'm never even taking an aspirin again." I sighed. "Why is everything in this world able to kill you?" I had seen a death by stiletto, gunshot, stabbing, and a fucking ice cube used to murder someone... I was starting to think that anything and everything could be used as a deadly weapon.

"We sent samples of all three cakes in, just in case. What concerns me is the time we have to work with," Sheriff Roy said from behind his desk. It was clean on any paperwork. Of course, it was. We were doing all the work.

Jensen glared over at him, and I noticed his hand slowly ball into a fist.

"We've interviewed quite a few people today." I felt like I needed to defend what Jensen and I were doing to the ungrateful man. We had given up our vacation to help him, and he wasn't making me feel very warm and fuzzy right now.

"Did you learn anything?" He asked hopefully.

"We can't say yet. Maybe... Maybe not." Jensen sighed and started reading the papers again.

"I have the mayor screaming and yelling at me." Roy pleaded.

"Sheriff... What else did you do today?" I snipped at him. He was really getting on my last gay nerve, and I couldn't afford that.

"I've been..."

"Exactly. We are doing our best. You need to get on the phone and call the FBI and see if we can get actual results.

We don't have time to wait since the coroner couldn't find anything in his autopsy, besides what looks like probable poisoning. That's a lot. That gives us a path to follow. Now call them and do your job, please!" Jensen grinned. He liked it when I got bitchy, but I wasn't about to sit here and let this man make us feel bad about not solving his fucking mystery in the first six hours of investigation.

"If there is poison in his system, it should show up in one or more of the samples I sent. Blood, mucous, the sick that smelled of sweet, or the organ samples that were sent. If it's there, they should find something that doesn't belong. If they find nothing, was there even a murder? It would be impossible to prove, I would think." The old coroner looked like he hoped this would be his last case. He had to be close to retirement age. He did have a very friendly demeanor and that grandfatherly vibe that made you want to like him.

"I'll make the call. I hate to push the Feds, but I'll call and plead. See if I can get a possible timeline that they might be able to let us know something. I did ask them to rush, and they said they would."

"Rushing to the FBI is very different than rushing to anyone else. They have a backlog over two months in most offices." Jensen stood up and walked over to the coroner. "What is this?"

The old man took the papers and handed them back. "Acne? Perhaps? It's hard to say."

"Cory, if anyone would have noticed, it would have been you. Did you see any acne on Alex's face when we met him?" Jensen turned to me. Sometimes it paid to be a fashionista who liked to look their best.

"Well, he had already been in makeup, but no. I mean, you can cover it, but if you look closely..."

"You definitely looked closely."

I pulled out my phone. "I have a photo."

"Perfect. Pull it up. Is there anything on his cheek?"

"Uh..." I scrolled. I took a few photos during the competition. "I just don't know what side of his face I got... Oh! Which side?"

"It was on the left side of his face, right above his cheekbone." The old coroner added.

"Yes! No... I don't see anything." I pinched the photo and made it larger, zooming in as tightly as I could on Alex's face. I did have a fucktabulous phone that had an excellent runway-ready camera. It's why I bought it. I took marvelous selfies. "Looks clear to me... Nothing that I can see."

"That's rather odd. But I did notice how heavy the makeup was on his face. Maybe he had a reaction." The old man sat down in one of the chairs opposite Roy. "I tell you... I think I am about ready to retire after this. The Pleasant isn't supposed to have this kind of thing happen here."

"Is there a poison that would do that, Jim?" Jensen asked slowly as he pondered the new information. I loved when he went into deep thought. He always it the inside of his cheek. It was adorable.

"Sure... I mean, there's a lot of stuff that could cause irritation that isn't a poison. But they didn't seem to be pustules. Something that strong... I mean, something that could kill you doesn't usually leave a rash. It causes blistering as the body tries to reject it. Those bumps didn't appear to be that. But it was something odd about the body, so I included it. I honestly think it's the wrong path to find what you're looking for." He slumped down in his chair. "Is there anything else, gentlemen? I am old and tired from pulling an all-nighter, and my wife is probably worried sick about me. I hadn't had to do that in a long time."

"I think that's it, Jim. You go home to Helen, and I'll let

you know if we find anything else that might need your eye." Roy sat back in his chair as if I hadn't given him his marching orders already. I kind of enjoyed bossing around a sheriff. I had practice with Jensen.

"Sheriff? The phone call. Now please." I smiled as sweetly as I could to stop myself from yelling.

"Just so you boys know. I sent my report to the FBI field office for them to look over – just in case, I missed something. But I don't think I did. Hopefully, the boys in Denver will be able to give you something that will put an end to all of this." Jim stood up from his chair and walked to the door. "Let me know if you have any other questions."

"Now what?" I turned to look at my handsome, almost hubby. He looked like he had been put through the wringer, but he was still super hot. I'd never seen him look any other way.

"I think we need to regroup. Think over everything we've learned and see if we're missing anything." Jensen stood up. "Sheriff, as soon as you hear from the FBI..."

"Of course." He pulled out his phone and stared at us. "Making the call now, Cory."

We walked out of the office and called Danny. He picked us up quickly, and we went back to his house. Jensen looked over our notes and started highlighting anything he found important. I pulled out my computer and started searching.

I googled the contestants first. Each one of them had been in Point Pleasant for a long time. Veronica had been a pharmacist. She would know poisons well. But what would be her motive? Money? That didn't seem to fit. Did the contestants even know that they would all win if the contest had to be called off? Unlikely. Who reads the fine print? Do you even know what is on your Verizon contract? Probably not.

Anne, like Veronica, had been born in this town. She had been the middle school librarian and had retired a few years ago. She had a Pinterest for pictures of her baking – a few recipes and a lot of her Border Collie named Fluff. Nine times she had won the bakeoff. From the pictures she had posted of her house – it was nice. She didn't seem to need to kill anyone to win. Besides, she had spent all of her life in this town.

Alex acted like he had never been here before. Why would Veronica or Anne have a grudge big enough to kill for?

Abigail was another story, but nothing very exciting. She had moved here after college from Vermont with her husband. He owned a building company. She started a business that made birthday cakes for kids… some graduation cakes, and what looked like a couple wedding cakes. But nothing in her history screamed killer – even if the last bite he ever ate was her cake. If there was something in that cake that killed Alex – some toxin or poison, there would be time enough to bring her in. But why would she have done it? It didn't make sense. Only serial killers murdered without reason. She had none. Even if her cake was what killed him, did she do it?

Once again, the question of motive left me empty-handed. None of these contestants had any reason to hate Alex unless they just really hated his TV show. That would be insane, and none of them seemed to fit that bill. These ladies were all off the rack and not runway. They were basic housewives with normal jobs and lives. If they were involved, I would bet it was not on their own account. Maybe they were used?

According to Michael, all of the ingredients were freshly procured and opened on site.

That didn't mean that someone could have tampered with them. We walked up onto that stage, and when we got there, perhaps we could have taken one of the ingredients and replaced it. Maybe added something else to it. There were no cameramen or lighting crew out front when we arrived. Anyone or everyone could have done something.

"Jensen? I hate to say this, but we may need to ask for the tapes. Do you remember if they used the same jars of flour and sugar and whatever else they used to bake their cakes?"

"I don't remember. Can we fast forward through it? I know that the station has the raw files. It was in their list of discovery." He called from the other room. I heard him set down his papers and the clips of his shoes on the hardwood floor. "What about the audience?"

"What about them? Oh…" It dawned on me. Vicki had written about this too.

"Exactly. What if the killer was in the audience, watching and waiting for the moment that Alex would keel over. Murderers tend to hang around and watch the aftermath if they think they can get away with it. It's like a game of cat and mouse to them."

"Murder in the Front Row. Vicki's first book had the killer watching the victim. It makes sense. Everyone signed a waiver for their image to be used before we could enter the tent."

"We didn't." Jensen looked perplexed.

"It was in the fine print of receiving a ticket. But we entered before everyone else did. They didn't ask us for our waiver. If they missed that, Jensen… I mean, we were in the front. If they missed that, what else did they miss?"

"Now that you say that. Let me call the sheriff and see if he has those files. I don't remember them on the list. Just the

A camera, which captured the full stage, was recorded in the notes. I'll see if he can contact production and get that sent to him today."

"Waiting! Why are we always waiting?"

"It's the job, babe."

"Hey." Danny walked into the kitchen that I was using for an office. The counter on the island was huge. "You hungry?"

"Starving," I answered quickly. My belly had been rumbling for hours.

"Can you take a break? It's almost happy hour, or are you in a place where we need to order takeout? I'm sorry about your vacation, guys. I had a lot of plans for us."

"I know. But that means we'll just have to come to visit again." Jensen replied. He seemed to really like Danny. They did have a lot in common.

"I think we could take a break. We might need to go to the office, though."

"Hopefully, we'll need to go to the office, he means. At this point..."

"Well, we need to watch the show and see if they have the audience entering. Danny, it might help us if you would watch with us."

"Oh, God, really? I'd rather be murdered, I think." He frowned. "Too soon?"

"Maybe just a little." I laughed. "Tom, baby. Will you call the sheriff while I go change clothes? I want to put on my cha-cha clothes. I really could use some food and a drink to take the edge off."

"Yeah. Sounds good."

"Perfect. I'm calling Crystal."

10

"Roy said he has all the footage. He didn't know how to put it down on the discovery. But he said the station only has a small television." Jensen slid his phone back into his pocket.

"Are they actual tapes?" Danny asked as he zoomed down the road way too fast for my taste. Weirdly, I trusted him much more than I normally did. There was just something about Danny that made you feel he was worthy.

"No digital files, I think. He said they were all on a thumb drive." Jensen snorted.

"We have a screening room at the house. It used to be my back porch, but Blake had it fixed up for movie nights. It will work perfectly, and the screen is huge."

"I'm not sure I'm ready to see myself in HD on a big screen." I groaned.

"Baby, you are always camera ready." Jensen turned around from the front seat and smiled sweetly. "I bet you even sparkle when the lights hit you."

"Only my jacket." I giggled.

"Ok, can he send the files over?" Danny asked. "We could hook up one of your laptops."

"No, the files have to stay on the thumb drive. Let me text Gates and see if they'll allow us to take them to your house. Maybe he'll deliver them to wherever we're going." Jensen's fingers started flying on his screen. "Where are we going?"

"We are going to one of my favorite places in The Pleasant – Liberties Pub. I invited a couple people, too. Everyone's heard Blake talk about you guys, and they're all dying to meet you."

"I hope not, literally. One mystery is enough, boo bear." I tried the cute name out on Danny. I saw him smile in the rearview.

"Boo bear? I like it."

"Gates will deliver." Jensen smiled as he slid his phone back into his pocket. "So, who's joining us?"

"Well, Blake is meeting us there, of course. Crystal has been texting me all day to see if you boys could get together. And then there's our friend Hart. His boyfriend is out of town, and he's been blue. I think you're all going to adore him." Danny turned into a small parking lot and slowly stopped his behemoth. Seriously, his car was huge. So was Danny. Between him, Jensen and Blake, they could pick up this car and carry it into a parking space. I guess I had a type.

I was just a twunk. That's a muscular twink for those who aren't in the know. I may have been a trainer and looked fabulous naked, but those boys were in a class of their own. Hopefully, this Hart wasn't another muscle boy who was so pretty it hurt to look at them.

We walked in, and people started yelling hi to Danny. It was a small town, and he must be quite popular. I mean, he was dating a movie star. But I bet Danny was popular before that. He was probably the all-star quarterback or some kind of butch shit like that.

"It's about time." Crystal cackled and threw back her red hair over her shoulder. "I'm so pissed off that you're slung up in our town's drama. I wanted to play." She pursed her lips, and I melted. She was the kind of fairy princess that every gay man should have. Gorgeous and obnoxious in the best way possible.

"Cory and Jensen, I'd like you to meet our friend Hart." A small boy turned around, smiling at us. He was adorable and a little younger than his friends. Either that or he had fabulous genetics – and... YASSSSS! He was as twinky as they came. I suddenly didn't feel so alone with these gym heads.

"I have heard so much about you. Cory, those shoes..." He looked up at me with awe. "Where the hell can I buy those?"

I posed, as one was inclined to do when someone said something flattering. "I had them custom-made in every color. I'll show you the website. They always have a great deal going on."

My sparkly tennis shoes had always been one of my signatures since I came out. Why wear something drab and boring when you can bring the disco everywhere you go? I hated the way I used to dress when I just tried to fit in. Now I wanted to stand out. It felt good to finally be comfortable in my own skin. It had taken a long time to get there.

"Girl, you better show me that website too. Hart can't steal all the spotlight." Crystal got out of her chair and gave me a hug. "I could just squeeze you and keep you in my pocket."

"I can't stay, but I hope to visit again sometime soon and not have to solve a murder."

"What?" Hart's eyes bulged out of his socket. "You didn't tell me that! Who died?"

"Dude? You own a bookstore. Don't you get the paper?" Danny chuckled as he waved at the bartender. "Hey, Lewis? Can we get three Redrums, please?"

"So you own a bookstore?" I tried to change the subject, but just like any good gay boy worth his salt, Hart wanted answers.

"Wait! Did you say murder?" Hart's jaw dropped open. He was so scrumptious I wanted to adopt him right there. The way his hair stuck up everywhere and those big black glasses that covered the prettiest of eyes was totally endearing.

"Yeah. One of the celeb chefs died right in front of our eyes, Hart." Crystal dropped her voice – thankfully.

"Holy shit! I'm so glad I couldn't go." He looked between us. "Which one of you is Vicki Dean's assistant? I'm a huge fan of hers."

"That would be me." I raised my hand.

"Wait. So it happened in front of you guys? Holy shit!" His ADD was causing me gay whiplash.

"Yes. He fell face first into a piece of cake. I am dying to ask you about..."

"We couldn't say a word," Jensen said seriously.

"Please, can we talk about anything else?" I took my beer from Danny and took a sip. It was delicious. "Wait, did you say Redrum was the name of this beer?"

"Oh... Yeah. Sorry." Danny grimaced.

"What's redrum? I don't taste any rum in this." Jensen scrunched his face up. "It's great for an amber ale, though."

"Spell it out backward." I huffed. "I swear I can't escape it."

Jensen did the math. "That is fucked."

"It comes from a hotel where The Shining was originally filmed. It's a staple in this bar." Danny smirked. "I suppose it's also very timely for you to be drinking right now."

"Is Vicki Dean as cool a person as she appears to be? I've been a huge fan of hers ever since her first book. They fly off the shelves at my shop." Hart looked up at me with those big round eyes.

"You own a bookstore? You seem so young. Was it a family store?" I sat down beside him while the other three started talking about something else. I honestly tuned them out. Here was another superfan of Vicki's, and I was excited to talk about something I loved too. Anything but this stupid case we couldn't figure out.

"Not really, but I've worked there for a long time. My boyfriend bought it for me. Have you ever heard of Lucas Morgan?"

"You mean the rock star? Duh! I used to have a huge crush on him." I looked at the boy with a new eye. Lucas was older than me, and I would wager a good decade or more older than Hart. He must have a thing for daddies or something.

"Yeah, that's him. He's on tour right now. But after we started dating, he bought the store for me to stop it from being taken over by a corporation and..."

"Are you serious? That's like right out of a Hallmark movie! Everything here reminds me of those types of movies."

"I guess. I mean, we are a small town that loves to celebrate any holiday that appears on the calendar. You should see what happens around here at Christmas. But yeah, he bought it for me. Do you think Vicki would ever come here to do a signing? I think I'd die."

"We could at least send you some signed books. We'll talk when I get back to Cali. She's as amazing as you think. She has uh... a lot of depth to her personality." And by depth, I meant that Vicki Dean was actually my best friend Victor Sommers, one-time hairdresser, and part-time drag queen.

"That would be amazing! Thank you." Hart was as sweet as he looked. We gossiped about the books we loved, and he asked me a few questions about some of Vicki's novels. He was whip-smart and as sweet as punch. After an hour of gossip and laughing, I was feeling refreshed and maybe a teeny tiny bit tipsy. Mama was used to bourbon and gin, so beer didn't do too much to me. I was what we called in the business, a professional bar fly.

Blake joined us, and our food arrived. I scarfed a burger and fries as if I hadn't seen food in over a decade. One doesn't keep muscle mass by not eating, and I had been feeling weak all day. Jensen was even hungrier than I was. He had two burgers. If I had done that, I would have had a food baby, and this outfit was way too tight for that.

"Gates!" Jensen waved at him, and he strode over with an envelope in his hands. "Are you still on duty?"

"Sadly. I'm pulling the late shift over at the tent. The tech arrived this afternoon and has collected samples from everywhere you asked. You might even have some answers by the end of the night. He's also testing any of the food items used. But he won't have that information until tomorrow at the earliest." Gates sighed and started to walk away before he turned back to us. "The Sheriff also forwarded you the information you had asked for from the production company. See you tomorrow."

"Those boys aren't used to this kind of schedule. It must be nice to live in a place where almost nothing bad happens." Jensen finished his beer. "Hey, Blake? Can we get a ride back to your place soon? We really need to go over all of this before we go to bed."

"Of course." Blake stood up. "Do you want another round, or should we call it a night?"

Jensen looked over at me and bit his lip, unsure of what I wanted.

"We should go." I saved him from himself. Usually, I would want to stay and play with our new friends, but there were only two of us, and we had a long night still ahead.

"Gates?" Jensen looked surprised by his return.

"We have a small situation. Press has been flooding into town this afternoon. It took them a while to get here, of course, being as remote as we are. But they must have followed me here looking for a story. They started taking pictures and asking questions as soon as I walked outside. Fucking vultures." He looked ashen. He had been taken by surprise and wasn't sure how he was supposed to handle it.

"Blake can't go out there." Jensen groaned.

"Give me your keys." Hart held out his hand. "I'll meet you out back. Cory? Would they know you?"

"I don't think so." I shrugged. "Maybe I'm a celebrity and didn't know it?" I winked at the young man, who was probably very close to my own age, but he still looked like a teenager. Yes – I was jealous.

"Give me your keys." Crystal demanded of Danny. "You've been photographed with Blake too many times. They'll swarm you if they recognize you. We can grab the cars and drive them to the back and then Hart and I can come back in and have another drink. I think we'll need it after this."

"Well, here goes nothing." Hart stood up and grabbed my hand. "Let's go. You can be my boyfriend."

Crystal followed behind us, and as soon as the doors opened, we heard the clicks and saw the flashes lighting up the dark parking lot.

"We're getting married!" Hart exclaimed. "Did you arrange all of this, honey?"

"Sorry!" Someone called out from the line people creating a barrier around the walkway. "We thought you were someone else."

"Maybe we are." Hart laid it on thick. I was impressed. "Maybe I'm the prince of Allyria."

"That would make you the king of Allyria, dumbass." Crystal smacked him on the ass. "Are you two good to drive home? I'm tired of babysitting."

"Yeah, we're fine. Thanks for coming to celebrate for us tonight." I gave her a quick hug. "Thanks, Crystal," I whispered in her ear.

"You two make the cutest couple, really." She beeped Danny's truck and crawled into it. I saw her trying to adjust the seats and hoped that no one else noticed.

Hart and I crawled into Blake's truck, and he started the engine quickly, siding forward so his feet could reach the pedals. Hart was quick on his feet, and without them, we would have a lot of trouble tonight. What would this mean for our investigation tomorrow? The Sheriff was going to have to make some kind of statement soon, or it was going to look like he had fucked up the whole investigation. I had learned that from watching how Harper ran the Maple Bay Sheriff's office.

But the reporters and photographers didn't give us a second glance as they kept their eyes focused on the front door. We pulled out and around to the back, where Blake,

Danny, and Jensen made a quick exit from the back door and slid into the waiting trucks.

Hart and Crystal entered back into the bar, and we drove away.

It was going to be a very long twenty-four hours. We had no idea how long.

11

"This used to be your back porch?" I looked at Blake's screening room with awe. The walls were covered in a deep green velvet, and the chairs were the kind that you found in the most expensive movie theatres in San Francisco. They laid back so you could put your feet up and had cup holders on either side. "This is amazing!"

"Blake had to have a place to watch himself," Danny teased as he threw his arm around his boyfriend. "He did build me a much better back porch with a deck that wraps around it. I really can't complain."

"Danny is not a movie person. Never has been, but he will watch one with me every now and then." Blake grinned and kissed Danny on the cheek.

"What are you watching first?" Danny crossed his arms. "I do not want to watch that competition again."

Jensen took the envelope out of his pocket and cracked the seal. He handed one of the thumb drives to Blake. "That's the camera A view. Let us look at that first. Trust me, we will be fast-forwarding until someone leaves their station. We just need to know if anything stands out now that we know to look for what we need to know."

"That's his long-winded way of saying – we have no idea what it is we're looking for." I giggled and instantly hiccupped. I put my hand over my mouth, and they all turned and grinned at me. "I rarely drink beer. Now you know why."

"Call me when you're ready to review the audience. I'll let you know if I see someone I don't know. Blake, would you know the people on the production team?" Danny stretched and slapped Blake on the back.

"Some of them, but not all. If we don't know them, just take a picture with your phone real quick, and we can send it to someone on the team to see if they're one of theirs."

"Oh!" I ran out of the room and grabbed my computer, and came back quickly. "I want to pull up the recipes and try to keep track if I can." I shrugged. "Sadly, I'm not much of a cook. But I can make a list." These boys and their macho-ness made me feel off kilter. Why was I always putting a lid on my fabulousness? I just couldn't imagine calling any of these people, girl. Or even bitch. Maybe Hart and I could have had that kind of relationship, but I didn't feel that with these three.

First off – I would never refer to my man as grrrrrrl. As much as I liked Dany and Blake, the moniker just seemed to not fit them. Did I fit them? Why was I spinning on something that didn't matter? They adored me. I knew that. They wouldn't spend as much time staying in touch with me if they didn't. It was all in my head, I was sure. Maybe one day, I would turn to Danny and call him bitch, in the same way I would with a lot of my other gay friends. It was an endearment only given to those you loved. It was a part of our culture that I fully embraced.

Shit.

I really needed therapy. It had helped Victor. Maybe I needed it too.

Blake, stuck in the thumb drive, turned back to us and grabbed the remote. "It's just like using a DVD or cable remote. If you need me, just scream my name. I'll come running. Would either of you like a cocktail?"

"Maybe after we finish this. I'm afraid I'll take a nap if I have a bourbon first." Jensen rolled his eyes.

Danny and Blake left us, and we sat down in the chairs. I instantly made my chair lean back, and the footstool slowly reclined up. I opened my computer and opened Jensen's email.

"Ok... I have the recipes pulled up. Let me move them over to Adobe, so I can mark them up. What exactly are we looking for besides anything that shouldn't be there?"

"Anything we missed, I guess. We wanted to see if they all used the same materials out of the same jars or... whatever they are." Jensen sounded anything but enthusiastic.

"You mean ingredients." I giggled.

Jensen hit play, and the stage appeared on Blake's large screen. It might have been the biggest TV I had ever seen in someone's home. The picture was crystal clear, and it felt much more like being in a movie theatre than in the back of Blake and Danny's house.

Jensen took control and sped the picture up. I had completely forgotten some of what we were watching. But sure enough, after the bakers were introduced, they went back to the pantry and got their share of the shared ingredients. Flour and sugar came from a large bin. Anne took the longest with each of the major ingredients.

But – and this was the not-so-fabulous reveal. The other ingredients that they needed were already placed at their stations on a large lazy Susan. Abigail pulled the leaves out from underneath her station. That's where they also got their mixers, bowls, and pans from. There must have been shelves on the other side. We didn't even think to look at that. But it made sense.

Abigail left her station. "Oh! I remember this. I thought she was about to assault that old woman with a rolling pin! Wait. Go back, honey. Play this in real-time. We need to hear what they're saying."

Jensen rewound to the moment that Abigail left her station and pushed play.

"Can I please get some of the cream of tartar, please?"

"I don't have it."

"It's there on the edge."

"Huh... I didn't see it there."

"Can I please have it?"

"Oh, that's right... You can't come in to my station. It must be weird having to follow the rules, huh? You were never very good at that."

"Ms. Lattice... Please?"

"Not used to saying that either, and I think I've heard three of them now."

"Pause it," I said.

"What the fuck is cream of tartar? Is that like a tartar sauce?" Jensen stood up and walked behind me to see what I was doing.

"Abigail's recipe is the only one that had cream of tartar. None of the others were using it. It's a powder. What was it doing over on Veronica's station, and why wasn't it on Abigail's. The ingredients were placed by the food assistants. Go back, baby, to when they first get to their stations."

I felt like this had to be important. If it wasn't, it was a big fuck up on the production's part.

Jensen sat back down and rewound quickly to the moment that the contestants arrived.

"There! Look. It's not on the lazy Susan with the other stuff. It's just sitting there on the edge." This was major. It was out of place, and that had to mean something. Someone put it there, and that someone might have put something else in it.

"How did Abigail know it was there?" Jensen stared over at me. I could see the wheels turning in his head. "Does she see it?" He fast-forwarded. Abigail did glance around. But she zeroed in on it rather quickly. "Did she just notice it? Or was it all a setup? A distraction?"

"Fast forward again." I sighed. More questions. No answers.

Blake started talking to them, and Jensen paused. "I guess we should watch this in real-time, huh?"

He spoke to Anne first. It seemed normal, as did she. Then he moved to Abigail. We listened closely, and as soon as she started explaining about the Pandam plant, both of our eyes lit up.

"Did she just say she brought these leaves with her from her own plant? She admitted that. I mean, that broke all the rules, right?" Jensen was in shock.

"It would appear to. How did the producers not catch that?" I gasped. "She admitted it to the host."

"First, the cream of tartar. Did I say that right?" I nodded to him. "Then the Pandam leaves. I think we have to move Abigail to a person of interest, and if the poison was found in any of those two ingredients…"

"It was her cake that Alex had just taken a bite of. But what kind of poison works that fucking fast. I mean, he just put the cake in his mouth and was talking about how good it was when he fell face first into it."

"The blisters on his face? Could that have been from the cake?" Jensen snapped his fingers.

"If it was, then Alex might not have been the target," I said seriously, realizing the truth of our possibility. "It could have been Anne or Gal. Maybe all three of them? But why? What would be her motive?"

Jensen thought about it for a second before answering. "She had been runner-up for the last few years. That couldn't be it. If it was that, then Anne would have been her target, and I don't think she would have done it during the competition."

I shook my head, trying to clear out the drama that was pounding at me. "It doesn't make sense, even if the pieces are all there. I mean, it's pointing to her, isn't it? But..."

"But the poison has to be there for any of this to matter. Maybe it's a coincidence, and maybe Abigail did cheat. Perhaps production told her she could use her own leaves if she wanted to. Maybe they didn't have fresh ones?"

"We'll have to ask about that. Were any of the leaves left for the FBI to test?"

Jensen looked at the list and frowned. "There were stems found at her station. They sent a sample, but... How could she have poisoned the leaves? Insecticide. A spray of some kind... I don't know enough about that to even... Are we in over our head?" Jensen dropped his voice to a whisper. He was scared that we wouldn't be able to solve this. Maybe he worried that it was always Harper and Vicki that seemed to break the case.

It had been playing in my head too. Jensen and I were the sidekicks to the main characters. Could we do this? I believed in him. It was myself that felt like dead weight.

We watched the rest of the show in silence until the

moment when Alex ate that fucking bite of cake. It happened quickly, but this time we saw him struggling.

"Go back to where Alex enters again. Did you notice that?" I asked quickly.

Jensen rewound. "There. The way he is pulling at the collar around his neck. Is he uncomfortable, or is something happening to him already, and it's working his way through him, and he hasn't realized it yet?" I pointed.

We watched.

"There. He's doing it again. He even popped his neck or stretched his neck. Maybe he was feeling the tightening of his windpipe or something." This was huge. This could mean that he was already feeling the effects. Maybe it was hitting him backstage, and Gal and Bobbi didn't notice. There was no way that they would have done it. They had nothing to gain.

Jensen narrowed his eyes. "It does look like something's happening. Hey, he just coughed."

"He coughed again. And now, after he takes the bite. His hand on his chest... then his neck... Turn it off, Jensen. I think we saw what we needed too." I scrunched down in the chair. Watching a man die in HD is not a fun experience.

"It doesn't appear to be the cake he ate. It looks like it was already affecting him."

"Did it happen backstage? Or was he already poisoned before he even got here? This... We have to wait and see what the lab tech finds. He..."

"Did the police get the garbage from the trashcans?" It dawned on me suddenly. The rash on his face. The moment we met him. Why hadn't I even thought of that?

"I don't know." Jensen looked at his list. "No, I don't think so."

"It's locked down, right? Gates is there?" I asked quickly.

"We have to go now. If what I think is there, we have to get it to the tech right away."

"Holy shit! The rash on his cheek... I totally forgot about that." Jensen jumped to his feet.

"Now, Jensen. Hopefully, the city hasn't already dumped the garbage cans around the tent."

"Danny? Can we borrow your car?" Jensen yelled as he ran into the other room. I closed my computer and followed.

Jensen drove like a bat out of hell. But if my theory was right. If my memory wasn't false. We might have figured out the how. Now, all we needed was the who and why.

12

Jensen pulled on the plastic gloves and reached down into the trashcan. It was right there sitting on top, along with some stems from the strawberries that they had eaten. Evidence that no one had thought about. The killer didn't think about this part of their plan. An unintended action that left a trace behind – discarded as an afterthought.

If we were right, and that was a very big if, this could be the smoking gun.

Jensen pulled it out and carefully placed it into the open evidence bag that Gates' was holding. With a quick swipe at the top of the bag, Gates' held it up and stared at it.

"Holy shit. You really think that this..."

"Maybe? We won't know until we have it tested. It might be nothing, but something in my gut tells me that they're going to find what we've been looking for on that."

Jensen ripped off his gloves and threw them down into the trashcan before he pulled out his phone and pressed the button.

"Sheriff? I..." Jensen paused. "Yes, we heard that the press was..." Jensen rolled his eyes. "He did? And?"

He listened and nodded as the Sheriff's tinny voice was loud enough that Jensen pulled the phone from his ear and put him on speaker.

"... and it was nothing, Jensen. All of the ingredients were clean. Everything that he tested had no trace of any kind of an outlier in its makeup. I'm... We have to figure this out so..."

"Sheriff... Roy... IS the tech still available?"

"He's in his makeshift office. He's checking his results from the autopsy. We should have something from them in the next hour or two, he said." Roy sounded like he was a straight man on the verge of a nervous breakdown.

"Gage is going to run something over to him at the lab. It's significant, and we need it done right now. Will you please call him and tell him that..."

"Now, listen, Jensen, I think you should tell me what it is that you..."

"All in good time, Roy. As soon as we are done here, Cory and I are coming over to the station. I'm afraid this might be an all-nighter if you get my drift."

Roy didn't speak for a few seconds as the enormity of what we were saying finally hit him. "That important, huh? For all of our sakes, I hope you're right."

"We are too. But we should have someone here with us as we continue our search. I just don't want to wait to get this tested. Is MacLeery around?"

"He's in the front office. I'll send him over right away." Roy wheezed.

"Make sure he has a full kit and brings it with him, please," Jensen said and hung up. We had wasted enough time, and Jensen was not one to suffer fools. He also hated talking on the telephone. He preferred texts.

I preferred his lips on mine, and no talking happening at all. That's how I best preferred to communicate. I was a sloppy gay when it came to my sexy, almost husband. He made me putty just by being in his vicinity.

"Let's check the rest of them. The only trashcans that had the contents taken were the ones onstage. So, let's see if there's anything else." Jensen walked past me and brushed his fingertips across my arm.

"What about an outside wedding?" I glanced around the tent. "It could be fun, maybe."

"These tents remind me of a ren faire." Jensen chuckled, reaching around me and taking me in his arms. "We do need to... uh... check these trashcans, and you're making me want to cuddle instead."

"Ren faire. Maybe I could dress as a princess, and you could be my shining knight." I teased. His hot breath on my neck made me shiver before he placed a single kiss on the nape. I folded into him as tightly as I could, pressing my body against his. "I think I'd look lovely in all that lace."

"You look lovely in anything and nothing... The sooner we get this done, the more nothing there can be." I almost fainted.

"Fine. You check the trash in the tent, and I'll walk around the edge and see if the city took the trash out there already." He slowly released me, and I looked over my shoulder at him, watching me as I walked away. I added a little extra hip action as I made my way out of the holding area and through the side flap.

I approached the first trash can and pulled on my gloves. I turned on my flashlight and peered down. Banana peels, some cans...

Shit!

I was going to have to reach down in there, wasn't I? I hadn't thought this through. I should have sent Jensen to check out these cans instead of myself. This looked gross.

I started pulling things out and checking each object out, just in case I found something that didn't look like it belonged. If I were right, maybe they disposed of the receptacle in here. Surely, they didn't still have it. They would want to get rid of it as soon as possible, wouldn't they?

Cans... bottles... a half-eaten turkey sandwich... Oh, God! I'm gonna puke.

I looked away and took a deep breath. My stomach rolled – threatening to unload the burger I had just enjoyed.

Get your shit together, bitch!

Vicki Dean would be standing in this trash up to her Victoria's Secret panties if she thought it would help the case. I am just as fucktastic as she is, in my own meager way. Think like Vicki and put on the big girl panties I deserve to wear.

I mean, I could tell myself this until the last call at a gay bar, but the problem was I didn't really believe it.

My stomach quietened with every piece of trash I forced myself to pull out and throw on the ground. Sanitation was going to hate me tomorrow. But it couldn't be helped. I had to push through this.

Nothing...

I shined my flashlight around and saw another large trash can about fifty feet away over by a bench in the middle of the park.

It's further away. Maybe it would have felt safer. I hurried over and shined my light down into it.

Oh, holy Rupaul! Ants... Fucking ants.

I pulled out the first piece of trash and shined my light on it before tossing it.

Newspaper...

Cans...

Oh! A bottle of Redrum that someone had...

Is that a... What the fuck is that?

I shined my light down into the trashcan, and there beside a takeout box, was a shiny piece of metal. The takeout box was removed and studied before being tossed aside.

Fucking werk that runway, bitch!

I reached down and pulled out a now dirty tube. Around the tube was a piece of... something...

Something with red on it.

Latex? Maybe? I held it up and carefully unrolled it.

Latex in the shape of something so familiar – something we all had – something that the tube was used to apply to.

A lip.

"Jensen!"

MacLeery arrived just in time, and we made our way back to the station with what was probably exactly what we needed.

13

It was definitely an all-nighter. With the findings from the FBI tech, we were finally able to find the cause of death of Alex Topacheffi, and it was heinous. A poison that was so lethal that even a tiny bit could cause death. Less than the size of a sesame seed is lethal, and when it is broken down into a liquid, a single drop can take a grown man out.

It even grows wild and is in family gardens all around the world. How many unknowing people had this plant and allowed their children to play around with it? Of course, I googled the shit out of it. The beautiful bell-like flowers were the main reason that people had them, and they were breathtaking – but deadly.

The Aconite plant, also called Wolfsbane, has been used for thousands of years as a neurotoxin. Oil from the plant can be spread on arrowheads and spears to take out an enemy. Assassins used it to deadly ends before the gun became the new way of disposing of an enemy. And apparently, it had been used, just as it had been on the emperor Claudius, as the tool to take Alex's life.

People read too many mysteries. Aconite has long been written about as a poison of choice because it used to be untraceable. Thankfully for us, it wasn't. The FBI found the toxin in their screening of the blood and tissue samples. It was a fast way to die. The dose was lethal, and he didn't suffer for long. If it hadn't been such a strong dilution of Wolfsbane, it would have been slower and much more painful.

I knew more about this than I wanted. I was going to have nightmares for weeks as I heard from the technician and googled the shit out of it.

Jensen finally got a call back from Alex's agent, who had stayed in Los Angeles. He didn't see a reason to come to Point Pleasant since he had enough to do with his client's untimely death back home. But he was able to shed some light, and finally, the pieces had fallen into place. A motive – a reason, even if it was a shitty one, to kill someone you knew.

It still didn't make sense to me. There was something else that we were missing. There had to be.

The Sheriff and his deputies went to collect our person of interest, and she was escorted into the room where we waited. The tube of lipstick and the latex used to administer the poison lay in front of us.

She noticed them as soon as she walked in, and her face went white.

"Have a seat, Sarah." Jensen didn't ask this time. His voice was firm and in control. Sarah slowly sat on the couch but looked anything but comfortable.

"Why am I back here? I... I told you every... everything I know." Her voice faltered. Her eyes darted between us, and the tube of lipstick that she knew pointed to her.

"I'm going to assume that the DNA found on the other

side of this latex is going to belong to you. We have enough here to charge you with the murder of Alex Topacheffi and send you away for a very long time." Jensen kept his hands in his lap as he explained calmly to her the situation she was now in. "You lied to us."

"I didn't lie. I told you the truth." Liar, liar, pants on fire.

"You told us half the truth. Maybe? Why did you do it, Sarah? After everything he had done for you, why would you turn on him like this? Did he refuse to pay for your son's master's degree?"

"No... Of course not. I... You have to understand the... I was in a... I didn't have a choice." She broke down and reached over for a tissue. I had a mind to get up and snatch them from her hands.

"What do you mean?" He asked quickly, not giving her a reprieve.

"I didn't know that I was... I didn't know it was going to... do that." She wiped at her eyes and blew her nose.

"Why? You had to have a reason. We have everything that we need, Sarah. Your fingerprints on the tube. Your DNA on the latex. We saw the lipstick marks on Alex's face ourselves when we met him before the show. We even have the napkin that was used to wipe them off. We have everything."

"You don't understand." She almost toppled over on the couch in a spasm of crocodile tears.

"Then tell us. Let us help you. If you know something more... You need to tell us," Jensen pleaded.

"I should get a lawyer." She sat up quickly and then dissolved again into a puddle of goo. Lord, she was a mess. Who wouldn't be when faced with the crime you committed?

"Yes, you should. But a lawyer isn't going to get you out

of this." I tried to sound sincere, but I think I came across bitchy. This had ruined my vacation, and I was pissed. I dug through the fucking trash!

"What did Alex do to you to make you turn against him?" Jensen raised his voice.

She wailed and rocked back and forth on the couch.

"Did he fire you? Did he do something that..."

"Oh, my son is going to... What is he going to do? To think?" She threw her head back and screamed.

"Did Alex do something to your son, Sarah?" Jensen dropped his voice.

"No! He would never! He... Oh, God."

Jensen slammed his hand on the table. "Why did you do it!"

"I did it to save my son!" She wailed.

"What does he have to do with it, Sarah! Tell me!"

"Alex was not what everyone assumed he was."

"But he had been good to you." Jensen reminded her.

"He was... But I didn't have a choice. He had done something to someone else, and... He knew about... He knew about it." Her sobs wracked her body like a hurricane. She was twerking on the couch as her fear ripped through her.

Jensen glanced at me as we watched her emotions roll through her. It was time to try something else.

"Sarah?" I said as gently as I could. "What did he know about? How is your son involved in this? Do we need to have the cops go find him?"

"No!" She sat up and shivered as her tears started to flow. She wanted to protect her son. She wiped her face with another tissue. "You can't take him. He had nothing to do with this."

"Is he in danger? If he is, you need to tell us." Jensen leaned forward.

"I don't... No... I don't think so."

"Then what? You have to tell us. If someone else is involved. If you were coerced, it would go a long way in your case. If You cooperate with us, then the judge will look kindly on that." Jensen was trying to reason with a woman in a spiral. It never worked.

"It won't matter. I did it, didn't I? I killed him, even if I didn't know that's what... It was supposed to just make him sick, and my end of the bargain would be complete. He said that if I... If I... did it, he would keep my secret."

"What secret?" He shouted again, frustrated at the circle this conversation was going in.

"If I tell you, will it get out? Can it be... kept?"

"I can't answer that, honestly. But Alex is dead, Sarah, and you were the one who did that. He was your friend. Doesn't the truth deserve to come out?"

"Not this. It would destroy him. He's already so fragile that... If you can... if it's at all possible, will you try to keep this off the record?"

"I can't promise that. It depends on what it is and how it ties to this case." Jensen's voice was so full of compassion that it broke my own heart.

"My son was not... I'm a single mother. I've raised Elliot alone since the day he was born. His father was a piece of shit who didn't want anything to do with him... Or me, once I got pregnant. He's always had a difficult time, my Elliot. He has trouble, you see, and always has. Once we got him diagnosed in high school with ADHD, it helped quite a bit, but by then, he was already running around with all of the wrong people."

She took a deep breath and sat back onto the couch, pulling her feet up underneath her and wrapping her hands around her knees as if she were trying to protect herself.

"He was a C student, most of the time. But because of his friends, his grades slipped. He was on track to graduate, but just barely. If I had left him to his own devices... if I hadn't pushed... He would never have been able to get into college, and he would have been on the same track as his father. A loser with no future. I couldn't let that happen to my son."

"One day, I was crying on set, and Alex brought me into his office. He asked me what was happening, and I told him about Elliot. He knew him, of course. We had been to Alex's house... He... He had been very good to us. He paid me more than the industry standard because the pay is shit for reality shows. He... He offered to help. He would make some phone calls, and... he did. He got my son enrolled at UCLA."

"Is this like the college admission scandal that just happened recently?"

"No... He didn't get a scholarship like those rich people. He... just got him in. His grades were not good enough, but with a large enough check from Alex for a new design building... They let him in. Alex paid for everything... But Elliot... If you knew him, you would understand. He's delicate and easily depressed. He has been his whole life, which is why he makes so many bad decisions."

"Wait. What he did wasn't really illegal, was it?" Jensen cut in, trying to understand. I admit my little twink brain was spinning, trying to keep up.

"No. It wasn't. But Elliot would never forgive me if he knew. It would be a scandal, of course. Celebrity chef buys poor kids way into college... But It would destroy him. He's been doing so well. He is still a C student, but this is his last year in college, and... He would never talk to me again. I know it because I know him. It would wound him deeply, and I'm afraid he would never recover."

I sat back in my chair and looked at her. She believed

with all her heart what she was saying. It would have totally been a scandal on a Hollywood Housewives level if this had gotten out. But it would have only been that. Just a scandal of another rich person using their money to get what they wanted. In this case, actually helping someone out that needed it. Not just another rich brat who thought they deserved something. This was more. This was compassion.

"So this person threatened to tell your son?" I asked. I understood. Love makes you do crazy shit.

"Yes. He would have leaked the story to the press. My son would have known, but... This person knows my son well. I was seeing him for over a year. My son likes him very much, and... I couldn't let him destroy everything... the only thing that I have. Can you understand that? I didn't know... Alex would die. I'm telling you the truth."

"I think it's time you tell us his name, don't you?" I nodded to her and got up from my seat, and went to sit beside her. I took her hand. "You need to tell us who tried to blackmail you. That's what he did. Do you understand that?

She nodded.

"Yes. You know him. He's the producer on this show."

14

"Cory? Can you hear me?" Jensen's voice was in my ear as I walked through the lobby of the Point Pleasant Chalet. It really was beautiful, but right now, I was shaking in my sparkly sneakers.

"Yes. Can you hear me?" I asked, trying my best to keep my voice calm instead of the hot, twinky mess I was actually feeling.

"Sure can. Good luck, and I love you."

"With all my heart."

I had never worn a wire before. Jensen thought trying to elicit a response, a motive from him before we brought him in, would be best. I was chosen because I was a celebrity whore and loved all things entertainment. Being a pop culture junkie apparently had its pitfalls.

We had enough on him with Sarah's admission. She laid it all out for us. But Alex's agent finally told us the truth about Michael Vickers and Alex's relationship. If we could get him to confess, it would go a long way in helping out the poor woman he used. He had told her that he loved her. He had treated her son with care and compassion. Then he turned and made her a murderer.

Michael deserved to go down.

And we knew where he was. He hadn't left the Chalet because of all the press outside waiting for one of the Hollywood types to show their face. Alex's death was causing a flurry of stories, and the speculation was quite the excitement.

One thing that I will say about this town. They kept their mouth's shut. Not one person that was there had yet to speak to the press. That was almost unbelievable. Most people wanted their fifteen minutes of fame, even if it was in describing the graphic detail of a grisly death. This town had closed its mouths and its doors to the press. I was impressed.

Jensen would follow behind me to Michael's door, and when we got what we needed, he and Gates would come in and arrest him. The sheriff and MacLeery were recording what we hoped would be his confession.

I had to screw my panties on straight to make sure I steered the conversation in the right direction. He couldn't see it coming? I just had a few more questions I needed to ask to tie everything up – That's what I was going to tell him. He seemed to like talking about his job and himself, so that's what I would use.

I had finally gotten to his hallway and...

His door opened, and he closed it behind him before turning to see me at the end of the hallway.

He took a moment and then smiled. "Cory, right?"

"HI, Michael." I forced myself to keep my voice steady. "I was coming to knock on your door. I was n the area talking to someone else, and I couldn't find your number."

"Well, here I am, I suppose. I was going down to have a

drink. This waiting around here is killing me." He ran his fingers through his hair. It was a little greasier than it had been. That probably came from all the sweating he was doing as he hoped to get away with murder. Killing someone was hard on the pores. All that fear ran rampant over your skin, and I was sure he'd have a zit outbreak because of it.

"Great. Just a few follow-ups, actually."

"Are we still being released tomorrow? I really have to get back to pre-production on my next show. Being stuck here longer than expected is causing delays for everyone." His portly frame meandered down the hallway towards me. "Hey! I was going to call the Sheriff about this, but maybe you can relay the message. He's going to have to do something about all the fucking press that's outside. We're never going to be able to leave if they swarm our cars. Maybe he can arrange our exit out the back or something?"

"Sure. I think that can be arranged. Hey! What's your new show?"

"Oh, I'm on a new cooking competition that brings all the network chefs in for head-to-head matches. Kind of like the NCAA tournament. Only one chef can be crowned the champion of all champions, you know?"

"Is that baseball or something?"

"Basketball. You're not a sports fan."

"Do the Oscars count? Cause if it does, I am a huge fan."

Michael laughed. He thought he had gotten away with it. He had completely let his guard down with me. Being a chatty Cathy sometimes is to my advantage.

"That sounds like fun. I can't wait to watch it. Will Gal and Bobbi be on it?'

"No. They are way too big for that. If they lost, it would

ding their reputations. All of those chefs have massive egos. Celebrity does that to you."

"So Alex wouldn't have been on it, either?"

"Oh, God, no. He has never competed on any of these shows. Not even when he was first starting out. It was always about him looking his best... or worst, which was what the public wanted from him. Alex knew his brand before anyone else did."

"Yeah. That's why it seemed weird that he was doing such a big pivot."

"What do you mean?"

"His new show that he was getting where he went into an amateur's home and helped them cook a meal. I mean, that's very off-brand for him, wasn't it?"

"Like I told you before, he did have another side to him."

"How did you come up with the idea?"

"Funny story about that, actually. My grandmother taught me how to cook, and I thought about the time I spent with her and how she helped me learn how to cut an onion and brown meat in a skillet. What if Alex, who really needed something that made him personable, went into people's homes and helped them make a meal for their families to enjoy. It was an instant... Ah..." His shoulders slumped.

"I didn't tell you that I had come up with the idea that Alex stole, did I?"

"I figured it had to be you. You seemed to be the idea man."

"Hmmm..." He ran his fingers through his hair again, trying to figure out what this meant. "You did, huh?"

I grinned as widely and innocently as I could. "Of course."

"I was pretty proud of it. I was pretty sad when after he

fired me, he pitched the idea as his own. But that shit happens all the time. They only care about themselves."

"You were hurt?"

"Hurt? No, I was pretty angry about it. But he wouldn't return one of my phone calls to talk to me about it. Alex was only out for Alex. He wouldn't even talk to me. Isn't that something?"

"He seemed to care a lot about Sarah, his makeup lady. I mean, he paid for her kid's tuition. That's pretty nice. How do you think her son would have felt if he knew the truth?"

Michael frowned and tensed.

"She told you? I... How could she do that?"

"You can't change someone's nature, Michael. You can threaten them, but in the end, the truth always comes out."

"I can't believe she would do that. That fucking..."

"I know you're not about to call the woman you professed to love and then blackmailed a bitch. Seems to me the only bitch here is you."

"He got what he deserved, and so did she. She cared more about Alex than she ever did me. She chose him after he stole my idea and cut me loose. She was going to stay with him."

"You turned her into a murderer."

"He trusted her. Besides, I didn't know it was going to kill him."

"And there it is. Did you all get that?"

"Loud and clear." Sheriff Roy said way too enthusiastically for my taste.

"You recorded that? Shit!"

Michael turned and started to walk quickly down the hallway as if he were trying to get away. Luckily he didn't apparently like to run.

Jensen stepped out from behind the corner and grabbed

him by the arm as he pushed him against the wall. "Michael Vickers, you are under arrest for the murder of Alex Topacheffi and the blackmail of Sarah Walton. You have the right to…"

I leaned against the wall and slumped down.

Some fucking vacation.

15

"Can we please go home now?" I put my hand on Jensen's arm as we lay in bed. "I need a staycation from my vacation."

Blake and Danny had taken us out to Rumors to celebrate. Gates even came in and had a few drinks with us. Hart and I exchanged numbers, and he promised to come to visit sometime soon. I liked him a lot and could see us actually having a real friendship come out of this. At least, I had that. Crystal gave me a big kiss and made a promise to come back when there wasn't a murder to solve.

I agreed.

They were all so nice and fun, and it felt easy to be around them.

"You did really great yesterday. Vicki would be very proud." Jensen pulled me closer to him, and I let my fingers trail down his hard chest – playing with the fine hair that grew there.

"You mean it?"

"Oh, baby. You were fucking extraordinary. But I always

think you are." He ran his fingers through my hair. "I wish you could see yourself the way I see you. There is no one else like you in the entire world. We're all lucky to have you in ours."

"We have to get up if we're catching that damn helicopter. I really need to shower."

"I like the way you smell." He kissed the top of my head.

"I like everything about you. I don't think I want to have our wedding in a tent, after all. Not after this." I chuckled.

"Yeah, I never want to see another tent again in my life."

"Hey! You didn't have to dig through the outside park garbage. That was disgusting. People are so fucking gross."

"Guys?" Danny knocked on the door.

"Come in," Jensen called after making sure the covers covered any of our naughty bits.

Danny opened the door and stuck his head in. "I have a total hangover this morning. But we need to leave in about thirty minutes if we're catching your ride." He grinned. "Good morning, by the way. You two look super cozy."

"You know it, sis." I giggled.

"Girl, please. We heard you through the walls." Danny giggled back, and then we all lost it. "I thought Jensen might be killing you. But you kept begging for more."

"I'm sorry that my idea for getting you hitched fell apart. It would have been fun."

"Next time. That means you just have to come back. You know I will need all the help I can get."

"And our stay is over!" Jensen sat up slowly. "We'll be ready. Cory has a very exciting ride ahead of him as we fly through the mountains."

"Jensen. I love you. But I will push you from the helicopter. You promised." I slapped his leg through the sheet that covered it.

"I always keep my promises."
Danny shut the door, and Jensen's lips found mine.
It was going to be a fabulous day.

The End

READ THE SERIES

Drag Queen Detective Series
Murder She Wrote... With Drag Queens! *On Kindle, Paperback and Audible. KU!*
mybook.to/DragDetectiveSeries

Men, Murder and Makeup #1- Victor has a secret identity, and she's being framed for murder. Will the hunky new sheriff help Victor prove Vicki's innocence or be a threat to not only his freedom but also his heart?
Divas, Death and Drag #2- A drag pageant where winning means not dying. It's a race against the clock to find out who wants the crown enough to commit murder.
Himbos, Homicide and Heels #3- Victor, Harper and Cory find themselves snowed in at a mountain cabin during a weekend getaway. Is there a killer trapped inside with them? The dead body seems to think so.
Exes, Extortion and Eyeliner #4- Someone knows Vickie Dean's secret and they want her to pay with her life! How far will they go to get what they want?
Sailors, Strangulation and Sunscreen #5- Victor and gang

go on a gay cruise. Everyone's having fun except for the corpse. Can they find the killer before they strike again?
"A good, old- fashioned murder mystery with a gay twist."
"One of my favorite series of 2021"
"A perfect 21st century version of the old TV classic cozies."
"Writing that just pulls you in-a five star read for me."
"I was blown away by what happened. Can't wait for the next one!"
"Funny, snarky and oh so hilarious."

ABOUT SHANE K MORTON

Shane lives in Studio city with his husband and their fur baby, Bette Davis. His novels include: The Trouble With Off-Campus Housing, Private Waterloos, The Year of the Cock, Fault Lines, Bluegrass Boys Series and The Point Pleasant Holiday Series. His Dark Romance books, written under Sean Azinsalt, include: It's in My Blood, Bound, Dark Eros. When not writing, Shane can usually be found at a film festival or performing cabaret in a dark dive bar.
Join Shane's Facebook Group- Sweet And Salty
Follow him on Bookbub- https://www.bookbub.com/profile/shane-k-morton

Made in the USA
Middletown, DE
22 September 2022